I let out a laugh as we watched the three of them vanish in the blink of an eye. Rita's black eyes found me and for a few heartbeats, we just stared at each other before laughing.

"I missed you," I said as I hugged her.

"Looks like I made it back just in time."

I pulled from her embrace and saw an expression of fear come across her face. Something I had never seen before.

"What's wrong? Did something happen?"

"Nothing. You should eat. I need to report in. We can talk later when I find you."

I did not pry, but I heard the hesitation in her voice and a pit formed in my stomach. Whatever it was, it had to be bad if it scared her.

I0676837

Praise for C. M. Hano

"It was amazing. This may be her first supernatural romance but I couldn't tell, I was hooked from the start. It is a fast-paced read that you don't want to put down. I thought I knew how it was going to end but I was wrong and I loved it. This is 18+ and stand-alone."
— *Viviana Five Stars*

Night & Day

by

C. M. Hano

This is a work of fiction. Names, characters, places, and incidents are either the product of the author's imagination or are used fictitiously, and any resemblance to actual persons living or dead, business establishments, events, or locales, is entirely coincidental.

Night & Day

COPYRIGHT © 2023 by C. M. Hano

All rights reserved. No part of this book may be used or reproduced in any manner whatsoever without written permission of the author or The Wild Rose Press, Inc. except in the case of brief quotations embodied in critical articles or reviews.
Contact Information: info@thewildrosepress.com

Cover Art by *Jennifer Greeff*

The Wild Rose Press, Inc.
PO Box 708
Adams Basin, NY 14410-0708
Visit us at www.thewildrosepress.com

Publishing History
First Edition, 2023
Trade Paperback ISBN 978-1-5092-4994-7
Digital ISBN 978-1-5092-4995-4

Published in the United States of America

Dedication

To the human I fell in love with.

Introduction

Present Day, New Orleans, Louisiana

The historians called them ghost stories, false truths, because they were beyond any human's wildest imagination, and because they didn't believe in the supernatural magic swirling all around them. But there is one story that remains true to this date. It can't be found in your local library or bookstore, only in a diary passed down with each descendant of Zirena, goddess of Night & Day.

The Prince and Skita had grown up in different parts of the Camilion, two more soldiers for the war, noble-born and placed within each household to learn to fight and survive, and to learn about the monsters on the other side. The Prince was tall and muscular, fierce but always smiling.

She knew she was different.

Hidden deep within the shadows of the Training Yard, listening to the adults' gossip, she heard a guard say, "She's an abomination. No Immortal should have tainted blood. Human and weak, like a chalice of blood turned cold."

"And so skinny!" another replied. "Never finishes her meals."

On the other side of the realm, the prince trained hard with his mentor, who exclaimed, "Where is your head at?"

"Are the Immortals all evil?"

"Of course they are."

"I'd like to see for myself someday."

They went back to sparring to finish training for the day.

A moment later, the prince whispered, "I don't think you really mean that."

"Nonsense!" the mentor hissed. But hidden behind the helm, the knight had his own doubts about the rumored creatures.

In the autumn, they endured long hours of training, followed by even longer hours of lessons in the stuffy training yards. When the humidity was at its worst, they escaped into the woods for a run or to admire the wildlife, but neither of them knew of the other's presence. Many times they crossed paths, but as the barrier fueled by witch magic kept the realms divided, so did it keep these two soul-bound lovers apart.

In the winter, the Masters left for their own training on the outskirts of the realm. As the days grew colder and longer, the mentors grew lax in their duties, preferring to sit inside or hunt for their prey. Bored and trapped inside, the prince worked on more healer skills. Assisting the palace healers, learning to suture and use herbal medicines for when the men returned injured or on the brink of death.

On the day the Matchmakers came to each of their realms, the prince and the Skita were lurking in the shadows of the corridors right outside of the throne halls, hoping to glimpse the gifted. Instead, the prince was taken by a maid to his quarters, while the Skita was sent to the training yard for another hour of endurance building.

The Skita's trainer emerged from the corner in her usual attire of a skintight black tunic and pants.

"Focus," Rita hissed.

"I am," said the Skita.

In an instant, Rita had struck the Skita across her face and was continuing her on-slot of punches, forcing the Skita to react and block each hit with her arms covering her face. This is how every day begins and ends for her.

The prince is scolded for being in the wrong place during important matters he is not privy to.

"Why must I always be sent to my room?" he asked the maid.

"It is what the King wants, milord," she answered while making his bed.

"Why do they want the Matchmaker here? What do they do?" His curious mind races with these questions each time they visit. No one has given him an answer until now.

"The Matchmakers are gifted. They can tell you who you are soul bound to be with by a look at your palm. Once you have found your match, no one can prevent you from being together. In this life or the afterlife," she said.

The prince pondered this.

The Skita continued to train.

With two souls separated by a wall of magic, raised to believe one is the enemy of the other, they grew into adults, training hard still to this day. Only the gods can determine if they will ever meet and, if they do, the dominos of destiny will fall and the lines of enemies will be blurred once and for all.

Part One—The Skita

Chapter 1

The courtyard has become a tangle of moisture and heat.

I was training my eyes on the thick male body before me, trying to predict his next move, which for a half-blood like me, was more difficult than I cared to admit. The shouting of crowds filled my ears, encouraging my assailant to break me in half, but I didn't dare put my fist down.

Anger has led me to this point. Fighting an Immortal twice as strong and quick as me. Being a half-blood is an abomination in these parts of the realm. The crowds have poured in, placing coins on the victor, leading me to believe that some, even a small fraction, may think I could win.

Improbable.

Blinking the sweat from my eyes, I brush loose charcoal strands from my face. Here, there is no one who I have considered as a friend—except for Rita. My mentor, trainer, and watcher, who forbade me never to agree to a fight without her present. It wasn't my fault that she was on a scouting mission, surveying the mortal realm of Camilion.

I shoved those thoughts from my mind. There was no time for distraction, as another thick fist thrust toward me. Dodging it, I rolled to the ground and then easily bounced back on my feet. My size was an advantage compared to his. With his back still turned to me, I jabbed my fingers at the pressure points Rita taught me and saw his limbs go limp before I kicked him in the face.

Although he is an Immortal, they still have certain nerve endings that could make them useless for a minute before their healing is complete. Our referee came to me, thrusting my arm in the air, declaring me the victor. There was no cheering, no smiles, only groans of disappointment.

I didn't let that pain show because none of them meant anything to me. Instead, I smiled and then excused myself from the training yard.

Only a few hours remained in the day, and I hoped Rita would return soon, but I knew it would not be until the sun had gone to sleep. Another disadvantage those Immortals had that I did not have was that they could not walk in the sun without being burned alive. The Coven tried to create magic that would protect them, but they had no success. I remember the days of testing. The horrendous screams of the volunteers echoed through the caverns.

Rita had caught me one day, and she scowled. Saying it was not safe for me to be out in the daylight. I didn't understand why she was so afraid of them finding out that I didn't get burned by the sun. Anytime I tried to ask her, she would just say it was not up for discussion or it was for my good. Whatever that meant.

It could be because if a mortal walking spotted me in the sun on this side of the boundary, they might suspect me as being a slave. The stories I had grown up with. The mortals spread lies about my people, saying they would bewitch mortals back into the caverns and then feed on them until they would turn them or kill them. It was barbaric. During all my years growing up in the Caverns, I never once laid eyes on a mortal.

Except for my reflection.

Every day I spent in the market, I would hear the whispers between the patrols to their mates about what they saw beyond the border. Rita told me to not believe a word any of them said because since the war ended, they had not laid eyes on any mortals. The invisible barrier the sorcerers conjured up had been working. I didn't dare ask what it was the mortals thought they were laying their eyes upon if they had ever come across it.

I longed for the day that I could join her and leave the inside of these obsidian walls. To smell something other than the dingy scent of wolfbane and musk. Wolfbane was meant to keep our other enemies at bay, and the musk was simply because of the unwashed bodies of the soldiers that trained. I had inherited the gift of heightened senses.

After a few minutes continuing to watch the defeated crowds leave the yard, I stood in front of the makeshift punching bag and started swinging. Though my body was still trying to recover from the fight, I punched to build my endurance. Being only half immortal, I did not heal as fast as them. The thudding of the thick bag echoed through the vacant yard, telling me I was alone again.

A feeling with which I was all too familiar.

I let out a grunt, stopped the bag in mid-swing, and leaned my forehead into it. The rough deer hide rubbed against my skin, wiping the sweat clean from my brow. *I don't think I will last another day in these forsaken halls.* Rita was the only family I have ever had. Leaving here would be a betrayal to her. I had only ever brought it up once, but she quickly silenced me before the conversation even began.

I stepped back from the worn-down bag and calmed my breathing, stretching my body out, making sure my muscles would not stiffen later. Yet another reminder that I was not a pureblood. They never became stiff. None of the lords knew what made up the other half of me. They just know that Lucan had gifted a mortal with me. He had woken, days before my birth, and informed the lords to retrieve me from the mortal world. Rita had led the party that night. I was born under a Blood Moon. Although a mortal woman birthed me, Lucan told them I was nothing like them.

So, what was I? Who was I?

I usually spent the other hours of my days in the library, studying the history of the world. Trying to find any clue who or what I was. I even dared approach the lords and asked them to contact Lucan, but they used the same excuse as always. Lucan would appear when he saw fit to do so. Rita told me he wasn't my father. I had no mother or father. They simply made me. She would not tell me why, and I assumed it was because she did not know. She had volunteered to be my Guardian.

I made my way to my quarters and filled a wooden basin with water that was warming by the fireplace. My muscles welcomed the heat. I took the lilac-scented soap and washed my body of the dried blood and sweat from the fight. My bruises, mere faint lines, have already completely healed. I dressed in my blue tunic, brown breeches, and leather boots, seething my daggers to my thighs. I braided my floor-length hair in two. It was the only way to keep my hair from getting in my way.

I had asked Rita if we should cut it, but she said it would be a sin because our god gifted it. Whatever that meant. She tried to explain that no Immortal could grow hair past their shoulders. That is why most of the women had shortened hair that made a small bun on the back of their head, or they cut it to the nape of their neck. Rita did not have hair on her head. Thought it to be a nuisance and too much like the mortals. Then she apologized, saying I was not to be offended by her disdain for hair. I laughed at that.

Down the cavern halls, I made my way to the dining room, where they placed deer and chicken on the table. Unlike me, the Immortals did not need to eat every day. They lived on blood alone, drinking from the animals they killed. I and the Coven needed to eat, or we would be famished. I have never tasted blood before. Never had the desire or need for it. Rita told me that was a blessing and a curse. I tried to sneak a drink from her chalice one night, but she caught me before it touched my lips. It would do more harm than good if I tasted it, she had said.

Her warning came from the wisdom of many years of dealing with the Conversion. Every time an Immortal reached the age of adolescence, they would need to feed. She said it took a month for them to control their bloodlust, and only the strongest of the Immortals could be with them during that time.

"Well, look who it is," said an annoyingly but familiar deepened voice. "The half-blooded champion. It is an honor to have the chosen one in our presence."

Demetrius.

I did not dare look at him. Nor want to acknowledge him.

"Don't be rude," His hot breath caressed the tip of my ear. "It arouses me, makes me want to taste you." Making a move against him would be against my better judgment, but my elbow moved on its own into his stomach. He did not even flinch. Grabbing my wrist before I could punch him, he said, "That was really naughty, Princess."

"Let go of me, Demetrius, and I'm not a princess." He sneered, exposing his pure white fangs, looking at me with his two black eyes. Confused by the adverse beauty of his appearance to the cruel intentions in the way he acts. Flawless, fair skin, high cheekbones, plump red lips, and shaggy black hair. If it were not for his perverted nature, the temptation would have won the many attempts of him trying to mate with me.

"What do you think, boys?" My gaze followed his. Simon and Tyler. Twins. Both blond, with bright blue eyes. A rarity amongst Immortals, another gift from our god, Lucan. Handsome, but not as eye-catching as Demetrius. By the smug smirk forming, it confirmed that he could hear the rising of my pulse as the anger within me increased. I hissed at them, baring my fangs. "How cute. Her pathetic excuse for fangs. They are not even real. I've heard they retract on their own. One of the many shortcomings of the other part of you, I'm sure."

"Let me go or there will be hell to pay."

He laughed, and it was insulting. Before my next word came to fruition or do anything further, hands ripped him away from me.

"What in the hell do you three think you are doing?" Rita admonished. She had come back, and I wanted to run up and hug her, but my feet did not dare move. "Shall this be reported to Lord Chaney?"

Demetrius's father and one of the lords within the Cavern. The three Immortals' eyes widen in fear. "No, please don't." The twins uttered, fear for my mentor apparent by the quivering of their lips.

"Cowards. Leave my sight before I decide not to be merciful." Rita threatened.

I let out a laugh as we watched the three of them vanish in the blink of an eye. Rita's black eyes found me and for a few heartbeats, we just stared at each other before laughing.

"I missed you," I said as she pulled me into her embrace.

"Looks like I made it back just in time." She winked.

I pulled from her embrace and saw an expression of fear come across her face. Something I had never seen before. And I don't like the gut-churning feeling it gave me.

"What's wrong? Did something happen?"

"Nothing. You should eat. They need me to report in. We can talk later when I find you."

I did not pry, but I heard the hesitation in her voice and a pit formed in my stomach. Whatever it was, it had to be bad if it scared her.

Chapter 2

Pacing in my room did not help the anxiety of waiting for Rita to come back so we could talk about whatever was wrong.

I wasn't sure I really wanted to know. Did a mortal see them? Was a person injured or killed? I should have prayed to Lucan more. I should be grateful Rita came back alive and unharmed. Something had to have happened for her to be acting like that. Hours passed since dinner, so instead of continually fretting about what could have happened, I left my room. Since the Moon was up and the Sun was asleep, I ran to the grounds.

The cool crisp winter air was welcoming after spending my day inside the hot cavern walls. When I first started running, the frosted air would burn my lungs, but eventually, my lungs got stronger. There was no choice but to adapt because of the constant frost and never-ending freezing temperatures. The Immortals, of course, are accustomed to it, because temperatures do not affect them at all. I was told it was another barrier to keep any wandering mortals from crossing over. They would freeze to death as soon as they stepped over. It sounded absurd, but the Witches swear by it. Calling it Frost Magic. Why didn't they use it to cool down the Caverns?

They found the Caverns underneath a dormant

volcano. A change of scenery, for me on my runs because although the snowfall caused a mist, it was a beautiful blend of black and white. Reminding me of the brackish fur upon many of the smaller creatures. Everything about our world was beautiful.

Except for those damned Caverns.

I took the same path each time—passed the east side of the Caverns, down the narrow path leading to the Hyperion Lake, around the Temple where Lucan slept, and back home. I stopped on the glistening marbled steps that flowed into the Temple. Rita told me never to step foot over the threshold because the god would ensure the intruder died a painful death. Another magic spell guarded it, and it made me wonder why none of us feared the Coven. If they were these all-magical beings, they could take over Alvion and rid us of them. Never did ask that question.

If Lucan were truly resting in there, my thoughts wandered into a fantasy realm where he would make an appearance to see his creation. Look upon the disappointment that I was. Not living up to any expectations he had. Although none were expressed by Rita or the council. Neither did anyone else, I presumed. The Temple had four ivory columns on either side of the vast stone doors. A patterned staircase extended from the threshold down to the obsidian floors. Sometimes, I did not want to go home. I would run up and down the stairs until my legs started screaming at me to stop, which was not until an hour or two later. One benefit of being half immortal.

There were just as many advantages as there were disadvantages to being who I was. Speed and strength were more than a mortal, but not as much as an

Immortal. My senses heightened. I could hear things over one-hundred yards away and could see in the dark. I could smell it from the same distance. I could not heal as fast as them, which, if I landed a fatal blow, that would not clot fast enough, I could bleed out and die. Unlike the Immortals, they could feed from each other and heal with a wound that bad. I could not drink from any of them.

Lord Chaney told me there was a certain level of intimacy that came with feeding from one another. If I were ever to be allowed to, or in a situation to need that blood, then whomever I fed from would be my mate for life. That bond was so intense, it often led to the pair having rigorous sex. He made it sound bad. Until the day came, I was to remain pure. I will be *Matched*. I dreaded that day.

Not because I was a virgin, but because there was no one in all Alvion that I was remotely interested in, and none were interested in me.

Except for that pervert, Demetrius.

I prayed they would not match me with him. *Dear Lucan, if you are my father, please find someone who is not like that pig.* I laugh at myself for believing a god would care about me or what I wanted. I did not even choose to be this way. He made me like this. I never got to choose anything for myself. Rita said I was the perfect warrior, and would be the perfect mate for someone because I was obedient. What choice did I have?

A crunching in the snow behind me caught my ears. Using my powers, I zeroed my gaze to see if it were a Snow Tiger or Deer, something that would make a substantial meal. What I saw was just as, if not more, mesmerizing than those magnificent beasts. Brown shaggy hair, deep green eyes like the beautiful evergreen trees, and a face full of hair matching his head. I could smell the scent of cooking spice coming off him and soaked it in. None of the Immortals smelled like that.

Their scent was bland and almost nonexistent. Or it was because I had grown up around it my entire life that I could not smell them.

He was not looking at me, but I could tell he was not an Immortal because his ears did not come to a point.

Human.

There is a human man in the forest. Near the Temple where my god slept.

I ran toward him, stopping before he could see me, and hid behind the enormous trunk of an evergreen. Crouching behind the branches, peering out at him, a part of me memorized everything about him. Wearing all black, complemented the bronzed color of his skin. He was the most beautiful thing I had ever seen in my entire life. And if I wanted to, I could kill him.

He would never see me before his neck snapped in my hands. I could hear the faint, calm beating of his heart. Confirming, he was oblivious to my presence. My sight zoomed in on the exposed skin of his neck, and the vein pulsating under it. My mouth watered and my heart was pounding with admiration and fear. I have never felt this...this desire and hunger all at the same time. He was so alluring; it was as if I was being drawn to him by an invisible tether.

I should kill him or take him prisoner and bring him back to be put on trial. But instead, my body remained put while my eyes watched him. Soaking in his very existence because he was not what I expected a mortal man, a human man, to look like. Not that I had any knowledge of what to expect besides the stories Rita told. Once, she told me that looking at them was like looking at Death himself. But I did not see or feel death. The only feeling I had was a desire to taste him. I readied myself to pounce, elongating my fangs, but something stopped me.

"Dean, we should head back now." There was another one. I did not see him. How was that possible? But the one named Dean looked in my direction. For a split second, it was as if he was looking right at me. If I was going to kill him, it had to be right now. My hands started tingling with the urge to grab him, but the pureness of him paralyzed me. The thickness of his jawline was hidden under a bush of brown hair, his deep emerald eyes locking, or appearing to lock into mine. I felt a furious rush from my head down my stomach and just below my navel.

"All right, I'm coming." That deep voice, authoritative, was even more alluring. He walked through the brush; the backside was just as enchanting as the front. My eyes trailed from the back of his head down to the tight, chiseled rear, and I felt damp between my thighs. Then, in two more breaths, he was gone.

Why didn't I kill him? My head slammed into the tree I had just used to shield myself. I truly did not know what had happened to me. It was like I was stunned in place and ready to lunge at him all at once. That has never happened to me before, not like this, and not around anyone here.

I ran back to the Caverns, not stopping to answer anyone's questions, and then slammed the doors to my room behind me.

"Hard run." I flinched at the voice coming from the chair at the back of my room.

"Rita, you startled me." Her eyes narrowed at me with a flash of worry.

"Did something happen on your run?"

Nothing I want to tell you. "No." That came just as easily as the prayer to Lucan that Rita would not notice.

"Good. I'm glad you are back because they're things we need to discuss." She sniffed. "I think you should bathe first. You smell like you ran for hours."

"I did." We both laughed, and the anxiety in my chest lessened. I took a quick bath, getting the hint that it would be one of her more serious talks. About what happened or almost happened with Demetrius and those boys.

Once finished drying, I threw on my silk robe and walked into my room. Rita was examining some parchments and switched her gaze to me. Her stare hardened onto me, halting my forward progression, not knowing if I did something wrong. My pulse increased. Her black glare went from the top of my head down to my toes, and a shiver rushed down my spine. Why was she looking at me like I was her next meal?

"Is something wrong, Rita?" She set the papers she had been looking at down on the small wooden desk usually used for drawing, stood up, and slowly walked...no, prowled toward me. She licked her lips, revealing her two sharpened fangs. I stepped backward, bumping into the wall. A sudden, icy chill snaked its way up my back. "Rita, what are you doing?"

"Do you know how beautiful you are, Zia?" She was inches away from me. My gaze met hers, and she was towering a foot or so above me.

"Thank you," I stammered, considering inching back, frightened of her. Truly scared of what she was intending to do. She reached a hand up to me, brushing away a strand of hair from my face. She cupped my chin and then hissed at me. "Rita, what's wrong with you? It's me, Zirena."

"I know exactly who you are, and I'm going to be the first to…" A loud banging from the other side of my door interrupted her, and I thanked Lucan. She was acting primal, nothing like her normal self. Something was wrong.

"Zirena, it's Lord Chaney. I need to speak to you if you are decent?" I let out a breath and was about to answer, but Rita clamped my mouth shut. "Open the door, Zirena."

Rita clicked her tongue.

"Is someone in there with you? We can smell fear radiating from the cracks in your door." Before either of us answered, my door was in splinters. Two guards rushed in. I freed myself from her grasp, and they pinned Rita to the ground. She fought claws and fangs.

"What's going on?" My voice croaked through my tears. Tears of fear and relief. Lord Chaney came in and then right behind him stood Demetrius. I hated he saw me like this. Scared of what was going to happen if they did not come in. Demetrius's gaze met mine, and then slowly flowed down my body. I looked down and did not realize my robe had gaped open, exposing half of my breast and then the very front of my body. He smiled at me, and I closed it tightly. "Perv," I shouted.

Lord Chaney smacked him right on the back of his head. "Foolish boy, show some respect for her and get her some clothes now." Demetrius obliged his Father's demands. Handing me a bundle of my clothes. I glanced over at the now unconscious body of my former mentor and guardian.

"What happened to her?" The question was verbalized twice but played on repeat in my head before I went to change.

"Get dressed, Zirena, there is much to be discussed."

Chapter 3

I'm not sure how I found myself outside the wooden doors leading into the Council Chambers. This only occurred when one was disobedient, which rarely ever happens. Because when it did, we did not receive just a lecture from the High Lords, but also a lashing. I still bear the scars from the last time. Although my body can heal itself now as an adult, before I reached adolescence, I did not have that power yet. Speaking up for myself against an instructor was forbidden. Even if my life was in danger. That day, out in the forest, we were learning how to hunt wildlife. I came across a nest of the deadliest vipers in all the realm. My instructor told me to pick one up and kill it. I told him I could not because one bite would kill me. It did not matter to them; they could get bitten and it would only hinder them for a day or two because all they needed was blood from another Immortal and it would cure them.

Unlike me.

It was just as forbidden now as it was back then for me to receive blood from anyone. When it got reported back to the High Lords that I had defied my orders, they gave me twenty-lashes and they did not hold back. Rita spent an entire week tending to my wounds with a potion the Coven had created for me. Not without argument. Rita threatened to decapitate them all if they did not oblige her demands. Which still brings to question why she was attacking me. The one person who had always taken care of me and tended to my every wound wanted to kill me and drink my blood.

I was so lost in my thoughts, I did not hear the footsteps coming from behind me. "You okay, Princess?"

"What?" I said, snapping out of my thoughts and turning to see two black eyes looking down at me.

"Wow." Demetrius let out a low whistle, surprised by the personal space he usually consumed. "What?" I asked, a little colder than I should have.

"I've never seen you so shaken up before." I was not sure whether that was a compliment. His forehead creased, eyes softening, the expression etched in sympathy and concern.

"I'm fine. Thank you for asking." He gave me a flat smile, and it made me realize this is the first actual conversation we have ever had. Without him making some inappropriate comment or touching me. "Do you know what's wrong with her?"

"No. But I know she isn't the only one." His voice was soft, and his eyes locked on me. They did not even dip once to look at my breast. He treated me as if I were a person. There was a mix of confusion and respect inside of me. I took a step forward, not sure why. I just wanted to hug him for his comment. When I feel like this, I usually sought comfort from Rita. That was not an option now. He stepped toward me, and we were now mere inches away from each other. We just stared for a few heartbeats, and I was not sure if I should just back away or reach out to him.

Anyone other than Rita, no one had hugged me. Demetrius only ever gripped my wrist or brushed up against me. His hands never touched where his eyes wandered. Right now, at this moment, he did not dare look away from my face. Heat formed in my body and flutters danced in my stomach. Not my usual reaction to him. This was new. "Can I? Hug you?"

His eyes widened in shock, and he just nodded. I wrapped my arms around him, burying my face into his chest, while his arms wrapped around my shoulders. I thought our embrace would disgust me, but I was not. I felt appreciation for him. The doors opened, and we stepped back from each other, locking eyes for a moment before someone ushered us inside. I wanted to thank him, but I did not get a chance before being seated in a wingback chair in front of the five lords. Demetrius stood to the right of his father. Smiling at me, and I flushed.

"Zirena," Lord Chaney spoke. "First, the council would like to offer its sincerest apologies for what occurred in your chambers. We detained General Rita for now and will interrogate her as soon as this meeting is over." I wanted to ask if they knew what had happened, but that would only lead to me being punished. I'm not allowed to speak during a meeting like this unless asked directly.

"I'm sure you have many questions to ask us, and we will answer them, but first we need to address the matter of your safety." I nodded in response, still not speaking, even though I wanted to. "The council has decided that you need protection and will assign a personal guard detail that will have a rotation of four guardsmen. We are all aware of your fighting skills and they are impressive, but because of your... circumstances, there are certain threats that you cannot shield yourself from."

Circumstance? Because I am not a pureblood, and I do not have the strength of Immortals, I am now defenseless. This is ridiculous. These thoughts never left my mouth, though. I just took a deep breath in and let it go.

"Demetrius and three others of his choosing will be on watch every other day. Escorting you to and from your lessons and even on your runs. Your routine will not change. You still need to be prepared for your Matching Ceremony. There will be extra eyes and swords surrounding you." He paused. "What do you think about this arrangement?"

A daring question and I could tell them all to shove it and just tell me what is wrong with Rita, but that would be incredibly stupid of me. I decided on another reasonable path. "My lords, I am incredibly grateful for your concern for my safety, and I look forward to this added level of protection." I took a deep breath, trying to keep my anger in check.

"Very well." He motioned toward the guards across the room, standing in front of other doors I had never seen before. My eyes widened when I saw just who was coming in through those doors. An iron collar around her neck and wrists brought tears to the back of my eyes. Rita, they have her chained like a common animal. When her eyes locked onto me, there was nothing warm about it. I still looked like her next meal, and she hissed at me. "Those mortals infected general Rita with some sort of poison. She and five others from the recent scouting mission engaged in a fight with them. They never saw the poison that was on the mortal blades. It took a couple of hours for it to manifest."

I still said nothing but blinked back the tears from my eyes. "There is no cure. The Coven has tried, but unfortunately, this bloodlust or primal instinct is their death sentence."

No, no, no, this cannot happen. Not to her. What am I supposed to do without her? I dropped from my chair onto my knees. I could not hold my tears in. I still said nothing and ensured my sobbing was nothing but muffled.

"Zirena, I understand what the General means to you, so I will excuse this behavior. You may say your goodbyes and Demetrius will escort you back to your chambers so you can start Morro. We will not disturb you for five days other than to bring food to you. I'm deeply sorry, Zirena." I looked up at Rita with tears in my eyes.

"Goodbye, Rita. Thank you for everything. May Lucan welcome you with open arms." I stood, and all I got from her was a hiss. Demetrius came to my side. I bowed before leaving and walked out of there with my head held high.

There were no words, no glances, nothing exchanged between us on the walk back to my room. Someone had already replaced my door. More than likely, some spell a member of the Coven used to create a new one. I reached for the knob, but before stepping inside, a flash of black passed me, grabbing me, and pulling me in. Before I knew it, the door locked, and I was back in Demetrius's arms. "I'm sorry, Princess."

He was genuine, and I did not pull away. Letting myself cry in his arms. The man who taunted me, bullied me, but always admitted how beautiful he thought I was had now become my place of comfort.

He held me for several minutes, placing his cheek on the top of my head. I took a step away from him. We locked gazes again. There was something different about him. I am not sure what it was, but he was not cold at my touch. He was warm. Safe even.

"Thank you, Demetrius." He nodded and then stepped to leave the room. "Who are you going to pick? To be my guards?"

"Don't worry, Princess. I'll keep you safe."

Chapter 4

Those five days I spent mostly curled up into a ball on my bed. I would sleep but not really eat, even when the guards tried to force me. Sometimes I felt a sudden brush of knuckles on my face and then a plea from Demetrius for me to eat. They burned and decapitated Rita alongside the other infected guards. Although Lord Chaney tried to prevent me from attending their funeral, I still heard their screams echoing through the halls of the caverns and in my head.

I had recurring nightmares of the attack and screams. Sometimes I woke myself up screaming, and Demetrius would run inside to check on me. He just held me, offering assurance that it was just a dream. I was safe. He was so sincere, and I was not sure if it was the exhaustion or trauma affecting me, but my feelings toward him were changing. The man I could not bear to be around, let alone touch, was the one I reached out to for comfort. Lord Chaney made an exception, saying if it did not lead to anything, Demetrius's hands remained from my shoulders up. It was more of a warning to his son than to me.

"Why are you being so nice to me?" I asked before I was finally ready to leave my chambers. We were packing for a run outside the Caverns. Lord Chaney agreed to it only because I now had four guards who were always keeping eyes and ears on me. He told me to not stray from the path and to not stay out for too long. Run to Lucan's Temple and then straight back. Demetrius and he had a private conversation just out of earshot. My senses have not really gotten back to normal since the incident with Rita, and I was not sure why. Lord Chaney also avoided answering my never-ending list of questions about why Rita wanted to kill me and what exactly made her do it.

I know he said it was poison invented by the mortals, but I just can't accept that for an answer. Rita was the best. There is no way a mortal could have gotten close enough to her to inject her with poison. None of this makes any sense to me.

Demetrius kept his distance since my nightmares seemed to fade out.

"It's my job now," he said with a strained face.

"Your job is to protect my body from harm, not my feelings." It was true. He did not have to be nice to me and hold me and comfort me when I had a nightmare. We were not that familiar with each other. We grew up here, but I cannot remember a time when we regarded each other as friends. "What happened to you?"

His face remained blank at my question, sending a surge of frustration through me. "Fine. If you do not want to tell me the real reason behind this newly found sense of respect, then I won't bother speaking with you about anything else."

"Zirena," he started, but I just pushed past him and headed straight out into the night. A chill circulated in the air. I was not keen on running at night, but since my guards were Immortals, they could not run during the daytime. Welcoming the much-needed distraction from everything, I knew the moment would not last. But, as the snow crunched beneath my feet, I ran harder and faster than I ever have before. Letting all the anger, regret, and sadness from the past week fuel me.

The distance between the two guards in front of me was decreasing with each stride, which only made me run faster. When I passed them, I smiled, letting out a laugh, and then kept running, faster, faster, until it felt like I was flying through the forest. My heart was racing. I could hear nothing above the pounding in my ears. The world slowed down around me. I could see the rabbit chewing on some grass to my right and, to my left, a beautiful white buck was grazing peacefully by a tree. Their fur matched the blanket of white that was all around us. Then I saw him.

Those deep green eyes seemed to focus solely on me. That feeling of desire plagued me, almost seizing me to a halt. There I was, standing right in front of him. Stunned in place, not sure what to do or say, whether I should scream for the guards. I raised my hand, wondering why the man, who I remember was called Dean, was not acting as if he could see me. This must be the barrier, which means he cannot see me. The thought crossed my mind, and my chest loosened a little. He was an extremely attractive mortal. My fingers tingle with the urge to touch his hair, his mouth, and his ears. To feel what it was like to touch one of them. Were they cold?

I took a deep breath in, trying to see if I could smell his scent again, but the barrier did its job that well. I got nothing but the smell of nature and a brief scent of leather and… death. The guards were looking for me and if they saw him, they would kill him. Why do I even care? I shouldn't because of what they did to

Rita. But what if he wasn't the one that did it? What if he does not even know about the poison? He isn't dressed like a soldier. Even in the mortal world, I can't imagine a soldier dressing in a red tunic, brown breeches, and leather boots with only a small dagger strapped to their sides.

Although I was told mortals are not very smart. Still, I cannot condemn him to the torture. They will sentence him without knowing if he handled Rita's death. I wanted to reach across the barrier and tell him to run, but I marked a tree nearby with an X, taking note that I would somehow come back here. I wanted to know why they hated us so much and why they killed her. After I made my mark, I took one last glimpse at him, so calm, so alluring, like he was studying the barrier. The guards were inching a little closer, so I ran.

I made it to the Temple by the time they caught up to me. "Where did you go? And since when did you run that fast?" I saw and heard the anger in Demetrius's question as he stormed toward me.

"I stuck with the path, and this is the first time I have ever been able to outrun an Immortal." That was half true. I did not want to tell him about who I saw because I know exactly what would happen if I did.

"Don't lie to me, Zirena."

"What gives you the right to accuse me of lying? It is not my fault that I out-ran you four. Instead of chasing down girls for play, you should've been training." I practically screamed in his face. I wanted him to feel my anger. It was not even about his accusation, but I was just angry at him, that mortal, the way my stomach surged at the sight of either of them. It was a mix of wrong and right. I despised Demetrius for as long as I could remember, but for some stupid reason, he changed the way he treated me. And it made my blood boil.

That mortal, the way he made me feel the first time I saw him here, in my land, it was just too much. I wished Rita were here. The thought forced a lump to swell in my throat. I wish…I just need to know what is going on and why no one is answering my questions. They had to know that I would find out. Even if it meant doing the forbidden.

"I meant no offense, Princess. We were just merely concerned for your safety." His voice and expression resonated with honesty.

"Don't call me Princess ever again." I glared at him, and he just responded with a nod.

Chapter 5

In my bed chambers later that evening, I sat at my study with my feather and ink pressed to a clean piece of parchment. I had the urge to draw, something I have not felt...since Rita. The image flowed from my brain to my hand as it moved. I made sure I did not forget the squareness of the jawline, the plumpness of the pink lips, and the perfectly shaped green eyes. Each line of his shaggy brown hair and scruffy beard brought a sense of wonder through me. Those perfectly rounded mortal ears, matching the equally perfect nose and smooth skin, had me blushing.

The loosely fitted tunic unbuttoned at the top, fine black hairs peeking out; something that would not fight the cold of Alvion and win. His broad shoulders, thick thighs, and calves show evidence of physical training. I don't know why I was drawing him. A mortal man, a killer, an enemy to my kind, my family. Why did I feel...a connection? Or I could consider it to be something, like that I guess. After I was done, I admired the image laying before, then lifted my gaze to the ones that had been collecting over the years. Wolves, deer, rabbits, and trees. Any kind of wildlife that I found beautiful; I drew it. The only other living thing I had ever drawn was Rita.

An image that was now a memorial of the woman who raised me. A tear fell from my left eye, and I wiped it away. A knock at my door snapped my attention. I fumbled with the parchment and then shoved it into my drawer. "Come in," I said with a pitch that was far too odd.

"Lord Chaney has requested a meeting." A guard named Alec, if I remembered correctly, stood there. I tried ignoring the flutter of disappointment that it was not Demetrius standing in front of me, but I just slammed that feeling down, deep down in that pit of despair. Alec had no hair. His eyes were a blue-gray that were illuminated in the lights, almost reminding me of the moon itself. His skin was unusually darker than the rest of the Immortals. I assume another blessing from the gods. Or at least that is what Rita always said if someone was born different.

"Is something wrong?" I asked.

"Nothing. But we should go." Alec's voice was firm but respectful. I got to my feet and followed him out into the hall. Each cavern hall was narrow, with not enough room for two people to fit through. So, the lords produced a rule to help with the flow. If you were not of high importance, such as a lord or a part of the Coven, you moved and let the more respectable person pass by. No matter who was walking toward me, I always moved out of the way. Rita told me I was higher born than most since Lucan created me. But I did not care about any title or the supposed title that brought me. I wanted to show everyone that I was not—

"Where is Demetrius?" I looked behind me, noticing he was not with the other three guards.

"Lord Chaney sent him on a private task," Alec plainly said.

"I'm assuming you do not know what it was

about?"

"Am I to assume that you miss his presence?" I said nothing. "I was told you two loathed each other, but maybe it's deeper than that. Maybe it's the loathing that is actually attraction." I stopped right in my tracks, turned toward him, and glared at him.

"How dare you? I never want to hear you say that to me again. Understand?" His eyes widened with shock, and the corners of his lips curled up in amusement. Then he just nodded. We were silent the rest of the walk to Lord Chaney's office.

When I walked inside, the lord was drinking from a crystal glass full of red iron, and standing to his right was his son. They paid no mind to me as I walked in and sat down in the chair in front of the wooden desk. I cleared my throat loud enough for them to notice me. I tried not to take their ignorance as an insult.

"Zirena, thank you for meeting with me on such short notice." Like I really had a choice in the matter. "I'm sure you have lots of questions and I am ready to answer them." Then I looked at the lord. I was not sure if this was a test because I could never speak freely at a meeting like this. Especially not in front of a lord.

"It's okay, Zirena." Demetrius shot me a smile and a nod. I was not sure where to start or what to ask first. Stunned momentarily by his presence and the never-ending cycle of what had occurred in my chambers constantly running through my head. There is so much to say, so much I need to know.

"What happened to Rita?" The first burning question blurted out. Lord Chaney shifted in his seat, both boney hands gripping the armchairs.

"We answered that the day of the Council."

"Forgive me, my lord." I paused and held my tongue, fearful I would say the wrong thing or make the incorrect gesture because of my emotional state at that moment.

"Go ahead, Zirena. I have permitted you to speak freely."

"Rita mentioned something that day of the incident…" I barely got the words out. "She said that she knew who I was, and acted like she wanted to—" I swallowed hard. "—drink my blood."

"It was the poison," the lord calmly stated.

"I understand, my lord, it's just… She said she wanted to be the first to taste my blood because she knew what I truly was." The lord went silent, and a nervous shiver ran down my spine. "She mentioned she needed to talk to me about important matters. Do you know what she was talking about?" Praying I didn't say the wrong thing, I felt it to my core that this conversation was going nowhere. Fear was rising inside of me because I truly did not know what this was about. If he was just going to avoid answering my questions or acting daft, then what was the point?

"Zirena, when you were born, it was with the blood of Lucan. He created you for a purpose, and because you have his blood and the blood of some other creature, it can make it irresistible. But only to those that haven't controlled their bloodlust." He paused and my heart was thrumming faster than it was before I sat in this extremely uncomfortable chair. "You know you will be matched soon." I nodded, and felt the sweat forming on my hands, but did not dare move them from where they lay folded on my lap.

"We have moved your Matching Ceremony up." I

sucked in a sharp breath, biting my tongue with the protest that was begging me to break free. "They are escorting you to the Castle of Alvion and there will be a ceremony at the end of two weeks' time." He waited for a reply.

"Who…" I swallowed. "Do you know who I am to be matched with?" Father and son exchanged glances, and anxiety and fear bellowing inside of me continued to boil. Please do not be him. Please, for the love of the gods, do not say his name.

"Demetrius has been matched."

"Demetrius." I gasped, and there was shock on both of their faces. "You matched me with your son? The one who before Rita nearly killed me, insulted, and nearly assaulted me every day of my life? Making me utterly miserable every time we were near each other. No. No, I won't do it." I saw the anger rising in the lord's eyes.

"This isn't up for debate."

"No. I will not go through with this. We are not matched." I stood up, standing my ground, and glaring at them both.

The lord got to his feet, placed both palms on his desk, and snarled at me. His very sharpened fangs elongated, displaying the menacing threat and harm they can do to me.

"You will not dishonor my son. There is no choice."

"I said—" I started, but the lord was in front of me in a blink of an eye. A hand gripped and squeezed tightly around my throat.

"Hush now, Zirena. My kindness only goes so far. Tomorrow, when the sun is gone, you, Demetrius, and the Royal Guard will head to the castle. The queen and king will expect your arrival four days from now. And when the ceremony is over, I will speak with my son so he can tell me how you tasted and what it felt like to be inside of a child born from the gods."

Nausea and bile crept up the inside of my throat. Hate for him consumed my emotions. My blood boiled with rage as if my insides were on fire. The room was silent except for the breathing between me and the lord.

"Father." I winced at Demetrius's voice. "If I may ask, please do not mess up her beautiful face. You know she doesn't have our speedy healing." As soon as my throat was free, my eyes shot darts of hatred at him.

"Get her back to her chambers and ensure she doesn't leave until tomorrow." My gaze never left the lord until Demetrius ushered me out of the room. As soon as we were in the hall, I placed my forearm to Demetrius's throat and used my other hand to pin him against the wall, while my knee was in between his thighs, ready to strike if necessary.

"Is this what our first night *matched* is going to be like?"

"Shut the fuck up. You do not get to speak to me. You don't get to touch me, and we will not be matched." He was not afraid of me at all. His expression was calm and full of admiration. Then I felt it. Pulsating on my knee. The hardened length of him. "Are you seriously aroused?"

"You tell me, Princess. Are you impressed?" he smugly said.

"You disgust me." I let my grip go and he followed in step behind me. I hastened my walk to my chambers and opened my door. Before I could step through the threshold, they pinned me to the wall beside it.

"Would you like some company tonight? Get a sneak peek at what is coming?"

"Let me go, Demetrius." He grinned. I knew struggling would be just a waste of time and energy. Making me realize he let me pin him to the wall outside the lord's office. He leaned into me, his lips brushing against my cheek and then to my ear. His breath was hot on me, and I hated the rush of arousal it brought me. My lack of experience told me that was what it had to be. There was heat and an aching feeling between my thighs.

"I'm sorry, Zirena. If there was something I could do, I would. I know you do not want me to be your match. If I could free you, without consequences, I would." My breathing relaxed at the whispers in my ears. I heard the truth in every word he spoke. And then a fearful, enticing, and irritating thought crossed my mind.

"Come in here." He looked at me with questions in his eyes as I glanced toward my room. "I want you to come into my chambers with me," I said, loud enough for Alec and the other guards to hear so they wouldn't disturb us. Without another second, we were in my room and the door locked.

"I know you didn't invite me in here for sex." I cringed at the word. "So, tell me."

"You said you would free me if you could." I paused, rubbing my arm, and then sat at my study while Demetrius sat on the edge of my bed. "When we leave tomorrow, something could go wrong and when we run, I could cross the barrier."

"No," he said, and stormed toward me, stopping

only a few feet in front of me. "As soon as you cross over, those barbaric savages will kill with no question. You may not like me, Zirena, but I will not let you run off to your death just because you don't want to be matched to me." I saw the faintest expression of hurt. I hurt him. He was angry and sad about me rejecting him.

"I'm sorry, Dem." A nickname I heard his friends call him. "What I said was out of anger for your father and the other lords. I just…" I paused and stood, pacing until I stopped in front of my window. "All my life, they have groomed me to be a warrior, not to be some wife. I could never choose a damn thing for myself. I have been obedient and untainted. Never tasted blood or felt another's touch. I cannot be matched because I don't want to be matched unless it is with someone I want." I heard the sharp intake of breath and felt my words stab him.

"I know I just insulted you again, Dem. But you tormented me for so long and then suddenly they assign you to my personal guard, and you turn into a respectable gentleman? It does not make a lick of sense. I don't know this man. You're trying to be well enough to agree to this union." I didn't want to look at him. I waited for a response and all I got was a door slammed behind me.

That was my answer.

Chapter 6

That night was full of anything but sleep. I was too anxious and angry at what had settled down. Something I was now regretting sitting atop my horse. I asked why we did not just walk or run to the castle, but the lord said it would not have been proper for us to arrive in such a schematic manner. So, he brought out the Night Riders, stallions of midnight hair, and the speed of a flock of birds. Another gift from the gods. No one except the guards and the lords could ever use the Night Riders, but this is cause for an exception.

The lord said the same thing about my wardrobe. They didn't permit my usual attire of a simple tunic, breeches, and boots. No, the lords had the tailors make me a proper wardrobe. When I protested that there were no other ladies, matched or none, that were forced to dress in such restrictive clothing—not to mention there was no place to strap my blades—that got me smacked, not on my face. Five lashings on my back for speaking against a lord.

If the crimson skintight dress was not already unbearable, the welts on my back made it worse. They would heal in a matter of hours. He made it to where I would feel them long enough to remember my place in this world. The corset of my dress was tight from my bodice to my waist and slit at both sides, revealing the full length of my legs. But not enough to reveal my two hidden daggers strapped to my inner thighs. I did not care what the lord said, it would dishonor the memory of Rita if I did not arm myself.

Remember the first lesson: go nowhere without a weapon, no matter what. My heart ached with the memory of her voice. I was in my tenth year of life, and she ensured I would have daggers small enough to conceal underneath any of my clothing, but still sharp enough to land a fatal blow. Ensure the blade pierces right below the ribs. That is what she said. I practiced those moves over and over until I mastered them. There would be no way anyone would suspect I had anything hidden under this. I fastened my hair like a double-braided crown on top of my head. To add to the illusion that I was some important lady in case we ran into trouble, my appearance would sway them.

What an irrational thought! I do not think anyone would look at me and think for one second, they should spare an attack on us. But if anyone were stupid enough to attack us, I would be ready. Almost praying someone would dare it. Despite the pain and exhaustion, I wanted to fight. The last one was when—

"Are you ready, Princess?" said that voice. I did not have to turn around to know who that was. Demetrius.

I prayed to Lucan that Demetrius will stay as far away from me as possible. Especially since he somehow convinced the lord to make him my matched. I hated him. All of them, no matter what he whispered in my ear. I cannot trust him or anyone else. They were hiding something from me, and I needed to find out what it was. My instincts were telling me this since the incident with Rita. I will find out what it is, but I would need to be tactful about it. So, I will start with the closest asset to the lords.

"I'm always ready," I said, letting a wicked smile of deceit cross my lips. He narrowed his dark brows at me with an inquiry. I just tilted my head to the side and gave him a flirtatious wink. If he were going to be my matched, playing the part would not be too difficult. He knows what the lords are trying to keep hidden and I am simply going to swoon my way into unlocking each one of them. Even if it means letting that filth of a man touch me.

"Remember, Zirena, straight to the castle. Do not stop for anyone or anything, no matter what. And need I remind you of what happens between two matched souls?" Yet again, he directed that question straight at his son. I smiled and continued to play along like a good, obedient girl. "May Lucan watch over you."

"Thank you, my lord." I nodded and then braced myself for even more discomfort this journey will bring. Two thick thighs braced on either side of my hips, a firm arm wrapped tightly around my waist, while the other gripped the reins.

"Are you comfortable?" His hot breath caressed my ear with his whisper. "Because I am." I wanted to answer that with an elbow to his gut, but his father was still watching, so I just leaned back against him, hard. His grunt brought joy to my ears. He loosened his grip on my waist, acknowledging he got the point.

Four to the front, four to the rear, and me in the middle with a guard tethered to my back. I glanced toward the north, toward the Castle of Alvion. My gaze shifted back toward the Caverns, a place I grew up, a place of memories with Rita, and the nightmares that had occurred. I scanned the entire forest around me, taking in the sights that were so familiar because once we started north, there would be nothing but an uncertain future for me.

Chapter 7

Within a few hours of our trek through the forest, my back healed and the exhaustion in my bones faded. There was little space between mine and Demetrius's bodies. It did not start out that way, because I scooted as far up on the saddle as I could without sitting on the Stallion's neck. Aware that the men traveling with us knew who I was, and the true purpose of this hastened journey, I sat straight and ignored Demetrius's arm wrapped tightly around my waist. But the Night Rider's reputation did not disappoint. Their hooves thundered fast through the brush, the clip-clop sound echoing all around us. I was not used to riding, so my body stiffened, and my joints were aching.

With each hour, my body scooted closer to him, until his chest was on my back, and I cradled my rear between his thighs.

The breeze was icy and pricked my skin. I kept the intended ruse up, letting myself settle in his arms. He did not seem to mind as his lips purposely grazed my cheek and ear now and then. He kept his hand loosely on my hip and it did not move, but I could feel the burning sensation rising in his fingertips at the want to move it. It brought a smile to my face at the thought of how much it tormented him to touch me but was unable to in the way he has always threatened to do before. I relished it. He would not claim or break me.

Because once we arrived at the castle, things would change.

I stared out at the vast, glistening blanket of snow across the land. Rita once told me, long ago, this land was of all kinds of species. But now, there was nothing but endless plains of snow, blooming evergreens, and flourishing bushes of greens. Something that would not have grown with a population of Immortals.

I was weary that it would haunt these lands by the death that continued to linger here. I let out a subtle, frustrated breath.

The Wolf packs and Mortals had destroyed these lands, tainting a once populace community with blood and decay, and slaughtering anyone who dared enter this territory.

And so close to the wall.

My eyes were strained looking for the hills that would lead us into the path toward the castle and I did not want to focus on the decreasing darkness night held and the vastly approaching day. We would need to stop soon. I would be the only one able to withstand the sunlight. But there was no way they would let me out of their sight. Especially him.

Demetrius.

The horses slowed, and Demetrius pulled me in closer to him before I felt the heat of his breath on my ear.

"Are you okay?" he asked.

"What's going on?" I asked, acting like I did not already know the answer to the question.

"We need to find shelter. It will be daylight soon and I personally would like to keep my skin intact." He chuckled and his fingers moved in a slow, gentle squeezing motion, sending a flash of heat through my body. I tightened my grip on the horn of the saddle, hating myself for feeling anything other than disgust with his touch.

"Are you famished?"

A genuine and considerate question that took me by surprise. This man was not the same man that gawked at my half-exposed naked body the day Rita attacked me. There was something vaguely different about him and I had a feeling it had to do with all the secrets the lords kept hiding from me. They only brought dried venison and cheese because like always, I could not, nor did I need to drink blood to survive, but meat, I needed that. Unlike them.

"I am fine until we find shelter." Both of us clearly ignored what his father ordered us not to do. But it was not our fault the sun was rising. I noticed the guards in the front veering off the path to the right, and I motioned my head toward them. "Have they found a place for us to stay?"

"No."

"Then why are they veering off the path?" My brows knitted.

"Because, Princess, this is Wolf territory."

Hearing this, my heartbeat increased slightly. I have never met them before, but I have heard of their vicious nature and their need for the taste of flesh. On some days, I saw what happened to the patrols that encountered them. Deep, horrific gashes with blood pooling the floors, bone sticking out from where a limb was torn clean off. There was no cure for a bite from them. It was like injecting poison into your blood. The only way to kill them was with steel blades to the heart.

Which proved difficult since you would have to be under them to even get close enough to accomplish the deed.

My fangs elongated out of pure instinct and then his hand moved from my hip to my stomach where my navel was and started moving a thumb in a soothing circular motion. "Easy, Princess." My fangs retracted, my anger and fear receding at the gentle touch on my lower stomach.

Another rush of heat thrummed through my very core, right where his hand rested so delicately. Why does his touch do that to me? My gaze blinked away from his hand and I strained my ears just so I can hear anything that sounded like a paw hitting the forest floor.

Nothing.

I heard nothing. Not animals. No bugs. It was as if every living creature within a one-yard radius vanished. And then I felt it.

Piercing pain sizzled through my left shoulder, the body behind me falling with me to the ground, anticipating the inevitable impact. My eyes widened as a scream of pain and terror rushed through my burning throat. I have never felt this panicked before. My skin was sweating and felt like I was on fire. A voice to my right was calling my name. Yelling at me to get on my feet and run. When my gaze met those dark eyes, I saw my fear reflecting on his face. His smooth hands cupped my cheeks, trying to speak to me, but I could say nothing.

I was stunned in place until I heard her. *Get up, Zia. Get up and fight.* Rita was speaking to me and, just like I did all my life, I obeyed. *That's my girl.* My eyes widened as I scanned the massacre playing out right in front of me. The screaming and whimpering coming from the massive beasts clawing and biting at the guards. There was an entire pack of them. Ruthless creatures, out on a mission of destruction.

Ten giant wolves with varying colors of fur, all the same size as the Night Riders. I looked for the one that shot me through the shoulder.

"Get out of here, Zirena."

That voice was yelling at me. Not Rita's, but still a familiar one, none the same. I looked at him. Demetrius. I spotted blood on his face. Fear was all I saw in his eyes, and concern—for me. This situation scared him. "Zirena, look at me."

I did as he asked.

"I need you to run."

"No." That response tore out of me with a fierce growl. My fangs elongated, and the fire in my veins from the pain turned into pure rage. Although I still had an arrow through my shoulder, I did not care. I pulled my daggers from my thighs and charged, attacking the first wolf that was biting into the neck of a guard. I lunged at it, slicing my daggers right through both sides of its thick rib cage, repeatedly, until I knew I had pierced its heart. It was yelping in pain as warm blood gushed out, soaking my flesh. I jumped to the next one. Stabbing, letting all that built-up anger and rage come out on them.

When I killed one more, I felt a hand on my right shoulder. I whirled on him. Pinning him to the back of a trunk, I could not see his face. My blood was pounding so hard in my ears, I could not see or hear past the rage. Then I saw it. That exposed and pulsating vein on his neck. Calling me, begging me to bite into it and taste the sinful blood. I answered that call.

Before my fangs pierced his flesh, strong arms thrust me back from him. "Zirena, it's over."

I hissed at him. Then, the pain came back to me in full force as the fire in my veins faded. The high emotion I was using to fuel my rage was evaporating. I dropped to my knees as the grip on my arms loosened. Then the flood of tears hit me as I saw it. It covered my hands in blood and fur of many colors, the arrow sticking out of my shoulder, and the gash of four claws across my abdomen. My vision started blurring as I saw him kneeling in front of me, telling me I was going to be okay. But then my world turned into darkness as the pain claimed me.

Chapter 8

Resting my head on the cool glass window facing out to the forest of sea green, my mouth still hurt with the pain of the fangs that wanted to break free but met with resistance.

I wish they would just go away entirely, but it was like an inner power lingering beneath my skin that blocked them out. Not that it was an unbearable pain. It was with every throb and ache, but it had been a week since the attack from the pack. I had felt nothing more than the pain, letting it overtake me because of what I did. What I had become out there in the forest.

Demetrius tried to speak to me. Convince me that what I did was okay and necessary for our survival. I slept for most of our time here, in a little cabin once owned by some farmer. The four remaining guards and Demetrius rotated their patrols and although Alec insisted we get moving, that we had wasted too much time, Demetrius said no. That I needed time. There was no way we could show up with me looking and acting the way I was.

He was right, of course. I did not tell him that, but I did not say a word the entire time. Eventually, I let Demetrius warm the wooden basin with water and he pleaded I wash up and change. He insisted it would make me feel better. Five days passed, and that water was cold with frost, and I was still wearing my ripped dress with an arrow still sticking out of my shoulder. I did not care that I smelled of blood and reeked like a dead dog. Did not care about the utter unpleasantness of my appearance.

Demetrius and the others did not dare touch me. I was yet again reminded that to be seen or touched until the Matching Ceremony goes against our beliefs. But I did not care. So, as I looked out onto the shirtless men sparing with each other, the first glint of emotion was raised in me at the sight of Demetrius's back muscles flexing with each move. Everything inside of me that loathed him dissipated during the past week. He had been patient, gentle, and respectful. He didn't force me to change or bathe. He did not force me to do anything but eat and drink. Told me I was being a stubborn ass, and he would not let me die from starvation.

My wounds had not healed all the way because I did not eat as much as I should've. They could not give me blood to heal faster because, yet again, I shouldn't be considering it. I did not let anyone touch the arrow because it was too painful. There was a vague memory of hearing Rita's voice during the attack. Urging me to fight. I could remember nothing but the pain, anger, and fire that was coursing inside of me. Demetrius and Alec tried to talk to me about what happened.

I was gone. My spirit had lifted from my body and disappeared. Until last night. When my typical nightmare turned into a dream. I was standing in a beautiful orchid of flowers that smelled of life. It was warm and welcoming as the sun's brilliance beamed down on me. Nothing like the cold I had grown used to. Laying down on my back, I soaked in the sun, wearing a god-awful-looking dress, when a warm hand touched my cheek. My gaze turned, and I saw him. A man I had never met before with midnight hair, deep green eyes, and plump lips. I wanted to ask who he was, but there was something about him that told me I had already known who he was.

He then leaned up onto his side, resting his head on the palm of his right hand while the left caressed my cheek. Leaning down, he brushed his soft lips across mine, and I did not stop him as the kiss deepened. I did not want the dream to fade away, but I awoke to Rita's voice telling me to find him.

He was my salvation.

My future.

My home.

Today, I look down at the man that was to be mine. I decided I would bathe and change into something more comfortable. Demetrius laid out a tunic and breeches for me I had hidden away in my sack. My hair was unmatted and braided in two, the tails of it brushing against my ankles. The arrow was pulled from my shoulder and bandaged with healing herbs that the Coven handed us. Knowing very well that something might happen and would require the use of them.

Today, I would speak to him, let him explain to me what happened, and then try to see the sense of why my feelings for him changed over the past two weeks.

For now, I'll simply watch him from the window on the second floor, laughing and smiling at Alec. They were both in incredible shape, enough to make me blush. I could not help but feel aroused at the sight of their bare skin. Wonder what it would be like to feel them pressed against mine. Then I wondered if Demetrius was the one from my dream. A kiss would tell me, and I contemplated it, but it would be entirely inappropriate until the Matching Ceremony. So, I just let the thought linger in anticipation. I laughed at myself because I was only regretting being matched before we started on this trip.

When their gazes turned up to me, I did not shy away. I just waved and smiled at them. They both smiled and waved back at me and then, in a blink of an eye, both were standing in my room. Still half-naked from the waist up. Sweat glinting off their skin and hair from their workout. "Are you okay?"

It was Demetrius who asked first. "Yes, thank you."

"You smell better and look better, too."

"Should I be insulted? Or thankful for your observation, Alec?" We looked and laughed at each other, and then Demetrius gave a glance toward Alec, and I realized it meant he wanted to speak to me in private. Once the door closed behind him, Demetrius ran a hand through his hair and down his neck. I bit my lip. Still confused by these newfound feelings.

"Zirena, are you okay?" That look of concern sent a fire through me, but it was not like the rage from before—it was the desire and longing for him to touch me. "Why are you looking at me like that?"

"Like what?" I teased as I stalked toward him.

"Like you are going to attack me." Because I am, I thought to myself.

"Tell me, Dem," I started, and then ran a teasing finger across his chest while I circled him. "When you saw me fighting, did you fear me?" I stopped right in front of him, inches away, as my gaze slowly went from his face down to his toes.

"No," he rasped out. I continued my teasing as I placed a finger on his jawline and traced the curve of his body down to his waistband. I felt him tensing with confusion and desire while my finger swirled at the edge of his waistband below his navel. "What are you doing?"

"Am I making you uncomfortable?" My finger remained on that spot, teasing in a circular motion, as his breath continued to skyrocket.

"This isn't right...we can't...Zirena." He grasped my shoulders, and my hands fell by my side. "What's happened to you? This is not who you are. You hate me, remember?" I felt that desire fade and then embarrassment flooded over me. I stepped back as soon as he released my shoulders from his grasp.

"I'm...I'm sorry, Demetrius. I don't know what's happening to me. I don't know what I am becoming." I started shaking.

"Zirena, when we were in the forest, you turned into something none of us had ever seen before in our entire lives." I sat at the edge of my bed, hands shaking, but he came over and sat across from me on a stool.

"What do you mean?" He looked hesitant to say anything as though if he spoke the truth, there would be no going back. Yet, I needed to know. "Tell me, Dem. Please."

"Your eyes turned to pure white, two horns grew from the sides of your head inches from your ears that shifted to a point. Then, on your back, you sprouted two large black wings that stretched ten feet wide and seven feet in height. They reminded me of the wings of a hawk, but more beautiful and more powerful. Your fangs elongated, and your nails turned into talons of black." I could not believe what he was saying until the flash of me looking down at my hands, the talons that were retracting into my skin, covered in blood.

"We were all stunned, including the pack, but we couldn't stop you. No one could. Three of them were on you, but even though they clawed and bit and tore at your flesh, you killed them. All of them. Your skin was on fire, and it burned through the throats of those wolves." Then that faint memory of burning flesh came back to me. I looked at him to see if there was any fear in his eyes. All I saw was sympathy and intrigue.

"Did I—" I swallowed the knot forming in my throat, "—did I hurt or kill any of us?"

"No." Then that memory of me pinning him to the tree and the strong desire to taste him flashed back.

"I almost bit you. But they pulled me off you before my fangs pierced your skin." I stood up and walked over to the window. My hand covered my mouth in disbelief and recollection. "Dem, what's happening to me?"

"I don't know, Z, but we will figure it out. But for now, are you ready to travel again?" Z, he made a nickname for me, and I could not help but feel the flutter of my heart. I turned toward him. He was still sitting on that chair, elbows resting on his knees. I wanted to apologize to him and make him understand that whatever was going on had nothing to do with these new feelings I had for him. They were real. Strong, and so I let myself feel them.

In a blink of an eye, I was in front of him, straddling his lap, my hands on the top of his shoulders. "What are you doing?"

I pressed a finger to his lip, leaned down, and

kissed him. Just like the man in my dream kissed me. His hands were on my hips and mine at the nape of his neck. My tongue pierced through him, scraping his sharpened teeth, and he moaned. My hips started rolling on the hardening length that was forming beneath his breeches. I wanted him. I needed him. I needed this, but he made a lot of teasing and perverted remarks. He never lied about the way kissing him would feel. He lifted onto his feet, bringing me with him as my legs wrapped tighter around him.

He placed me gently on the bed as my hands traced the outlines of his muscled chest. This kiss was full of passion and desire. No denying it. An arm under my shoulders, the other on my neck, daring, begging for permission to explore. I grabbed his hand and lowered it to my breast, and his body shuddered above me. He squeezed it while his thumb played with the hardened tip of my breast and my hands played with the waistband of his breeches. He stilled before me and released his kiss from me. I didn't want to stop. I didn't care if we had not gone through with the ceremony. With all the pain and anger I had experienced these past two weeks, I wanted to feel good. I needed a release and a distraction.

"Z," he started, then pressed his brow into me, inhaling my scent, "Tell me to stop."

"I can't," I rasped, pulling him closer to me.

"No matter how badly I want this, and trust me, I do, it is not right. Lucan will strike me down if I take you before the Ceremony." I giggled and then my hand traveled lower. I dared to touch the full length of his hardness. Teasing it underneath the cloth of his breeches, rubbing up and down, feeling him get harder.

*I wanted to know what it felt like touching skin to skin.
"You aren't making this easy by touching me like that."*

*"I don't care," I said, and I rubbed him harder
and faster. He moaned in approval. I had no clue
whether I was doing it correctly. He kissed me again
and then his hand trailed from my breast down to where
my tunic met my waistband. Lifting it just enough for
him to place his hand on my bare skin. Desire ignited
even more. He sat me up and pulled my tunic off me
when a knock sounded from outside the door.*

*"Dem." It was Alec, and I watched as the
disappointment lurched on Demetrius's face. "Is
everything all right?"*

*I smiled at him as he let my tunic fall back down,
placing his hands on my hips with mine on his
shoulders.*

"It's okay," I told him.

*"It's probably for the best," he whispered and then
kissed my brow before leaving me to go speak with
Alec. Then a wicked and sinful thought crossed my
mind as I peeked out at the other guard. What would it
be like to have both kissing me? I thought. When the
door closed, Demetrius turned to me, running his hand
through his hair as he slowly approached where I sat
on the bed.*

"What was that about?" I asked.

*"Just a reminder of what our mission is and to stop
doing whatever it is we were doing before we get us
damned by the gods." I flushed but not from
embarrassment, but at the thought of Alec knowing
what we were just doing in here.*

*"Oh, and what is that?" I teasingly asked while I
approached him. I chewed on my lower lip at the very*

sight of him.

"If you keep looking at me like that, I won't stop when the next interruption happens." I pray you do not. "As much as I enjoyed what happened, we can't go any further and we can't do that again."

"Is that what you really want?" A daring question posed as I stepped closer to him. Anticipating his answer as I unlaced the top of my tunic. "From what I can see," —my eyes glanced down at the bulge in his breeches.— "You want to take me to the bed and do exactly what you threatened to do so many times before?"

He blushed, and I saw him gulp down as my tunic fell to the floor and I stood naked from the waist up. "Nothing to say?"

"No." He rushed to me, kissing me, not caring what the gods would think. If we were to be matched anyway, why should we wait? He was my first kiss, my first touch, and it felt good. He ripped my breeches from me, and I did the same to him. The length of him pressed against my thigh as he laid us down on the bed. This was it. Damn the consequences because Demetrius wanted me despite what he saw me turn into. I wanted him. He looked at me and then he kissed me again, then my neck, those fangs scraping against my skin, down to my breast, nipping at the tip, sending an electrifying surge of desire through me.

His hands wandered down between my thighs, cupping me. My back arched in response and I moaned into his mouth. His thumb swirled in tiny, teasing circles at that overly sensitive bundle of nerves I never knew about. Then he plunged a finger inside me, pumping it in and out and then another one. I was nearly screaming at the sensation it rose within me. My hand curled around his slick hardness, and I started thrumming it up and down. The faster he went, the faster my hand manipulated his cock, and we were in a fit of passion. Longing. Desire.

I placed his tip at the edge of my entrance and swirled it around the wetness of it. I bit his lip and moaned.

My hands found themselves on either side of his ass, and I pushed him inside of me. Ignoring the burning pain that started and then soon vanished, turning into undeniable pleasure.

"Fuck," he barely breathed out.

When the full length of him seethed deep inside of me, my hips rolled, begging him to move. He obliged, and he thrust inside of me, slow and steady. Like I imagined a lover would do. But I did not want that. I wanted him to fuck me hard and fast.

"Please," I begged.

"What do you want, Z?" he asked in between kisses.

"I want you hard and fast. Now!"

He obliged me again.

Then I felt it. The climax and throbbing built and increased with each thrust in and out. Then, when I thought I could not handle it anymore, his thumb danced around that center of me, and release shuddered through my body and gushed all over him. He found his release at the same time, roaring so loud I was sure all the guards, including Alec, now knew exactly what was going on in here.

We stared at each other with nothing but breath exchanged between us and our perspired skin. He kissed my brow and then eased out of me, but not going too far away. His arm was under my shoulders while the other draped across my waist. His leg lay between my legs, and he smiled at me while toiling with a loose strand of my hair.

"Dem," I started, and he just quieted me with a kiss.

"I know," was all he said. But I was not sure if he did. I wanted to tell him that this was real for me, and I wanted to know if it was for him. I needed to know that this was not just him fulfilling his wishes and desires of taking me to his bed.

"Is this real?" I finally asked.

"Yes, Princess," he answered. "As real as any dream you have." And then it donned on me the moment my eyes flooded open.

It was a dream. I threw the blankets off me and looked down to see if I was bleeding. Rita had told me this typically happened once you had sex for the first time. There was nothing there, and Demetrius and Alec were nowhere to be seen. I had a sex dream about him. Oh gods, what is wrong with me?

But then what about what he told me I shifted into? Was that true? I did not waste another moment thinking, so I washed the wetness from all parts of me, especially the result of that damned dream I had, and dressed.

I found Demetrius and Alec deep in conversation. My cheeks heated at the sight of them both. Especially from the thoughts I had about sharing a bed with both at the same time. I stepped down, not acknowledging them, and took some bread from the center of the wooden table. They did not so much as acknowledge me, either. So, I cleared my throat.

"Look who finally made her way down," Alec said as they turned to me.

"Did you sleep well?" Demetrius asked. I swallowed back the heat trying to break free.

"Very well, thank you."

"Because we heard some strange noises coming from your room," Alec teased, and then embarrassment hit me, watching his smirk grow wider.

"What noises?" I tried to play it off.

"Moaning and rasping. It was almost like you were hav—"

"Shut it," I yelled before he could finish that sentence.

"Oh, my. I wonder who she was dreaming about that caused her to moan like that?" Alec said.

"Get out." Demetrius's tone surprised me. There was a hint of anger and disgust in his voice directed at Alec.

"All right, I meant no offense." Alec got to his feet and left but stopped to say, "If I hear those noises again, should I come in?" I threw the bread I had been nibbling on right at his head.

"Sorry about him," Dem said."

"What happened to me in the forest?" I asked, dodging that conversation further.

"You don't remember?" He arched an eyebrow, staring and waiting for my response.

"Clearly, if I remembered then I wouldn't be asking you now, would I?" My tone was sharp and cool. I did not care, though.

"You changed." He told me exactly what he had said to me in my dream. There was nothing but the flicking of flames when the conversation was over.

Chapter 9

I spent the rest of the day inside my room, letting all the events of the past weeks steal my sleep from me yet again. Still angry and ashamed of what I dreamed about.

There was no way I could ever, nor will ever, let that happen. No matter how good it felt in my dream, I did not recognize myself at all. That was not real. I tried to convince myself over and over that I would not be damned by the gods for simply having a dream like that. Although Demetrius changed in more ways than one since becoming my guard, I still could not get past that utter hate and memories of the harassment over the years. The way he relished in my embarrassment when my robe split in two the night of the attack. Bile crept up in my throat. This. This was the normal reaction I had to him, not some need and desire.

I was determined to stay as professional around him as possible, in the same manner as everyone else. With my chin held up high, I addressed everyone appropriately and ignored that tall, dark-haired brute. I had not spoken a word to him since he told me, well, confirmed everything that I had dreamed about with my change. I could not bring myself to be around him because part of me always wanted to hit him and the other. Oh, gods, it was a flush of heat with the memory of that dream. I wondered if this was typical for matched souls to have these sorts of wants and desires so close to the Ceremony. Lucan had sent me that dream to remind me of my duties and then, because I ignored him, made the dream feel all too real.

I did not want to be matched. Did not want to live a life of being bound to someone I did not really know or love. Regardless of the flirtatious glances and the change in his personality, I still did not want to be with him for the rest of my life. But as soon as we arrive, later than expected, might I add, the Queen will surely have the Ceremony moved up, and I will no longer be free. Not that I have been free since birth.

Would the guards tell the Queen what happened? What have I changed into? If so, what would happen to me?

A knock at my door brought me out of my head. "Enter."

"We are heading out in a few minutes." There was a mix of emotions when I laid my eyes on Alec. Relief and disappointment the strongest.

"I will be out in a few moments." He nodded in acknowledgment and gently closed the door behind him. Quickly, I dressed in a clean ivory tunic, brown breeches, and black leather boots, with some knee-high socks to help aid against the cold. I braided my hair in its typical style, tails flushed with my ankles. My two daggers were strapped to the outside of my thighs. There was no need to hide my weapons any longer.

I took one last glance at the wooden cabin, soaking in the last taste of freedom it offered me, and then mounted my horse. Unfortunately, there were only three Night Riders left since the attack. So, the guards took turns riding or walking the rest of the way. We still would not arrive for another two days, and everyone was on high alert in case another pack was going to attack. I still vaguely remember what occurred during it. Rita's voice rang in my ears, telling me to fight. The smell of blood and the feel of fur stuck on my skin. The memory of sharp black talons and a set of wings bursting from my body.

I still could not believe it, nor understand why or how no one knew about this sooner. Or they did but decided it was best not to say anything. That was what Rita was trying to tell me before that poison made her turn into a monster. If she knew and the lords knew, what if they found out she wanted to tell me, and they poisoned her? Shut up, I told myself. There was no point in developing accusations as outrageous as those. They said the mortals did it and so it had to be true.

That image of the mortal man came flooding back to me. The feelings that came to me when I saw him. That dream about Demetrius was nothing but lust and curiosity; quite different from when I was in the presence of that man. When I was mere inches away from soaking in his scent, and the need to taste him, caused my fangs to elongate. Just the memory of him was making them move. I resisted it.

Something I had mastered since they first appeared when I was in my tenth year of life. Rita had me practicing elongating and retracting them until I mastered them and was in full control. At first, there was a tearing, burning, and stabbing pain and the taste of my blood. After a few months, it soon became second nature. Unless I was angry or in a fit of rage. Then I had no control of them when that happened, and Rita told me it was because of the ancestors in their primal days, where they ruled by blood and blood alone.

"Are you okay?" Demetrius rode up to my left side.

"Yes." I didn't bother to look at him directly, but from my peripheral vision noticed a slight burrow in his brows with confusion and disbelief.

"You haven't spoken or looked at me since I told you what happened during the attack." He was right. But it had nothing to do with that conversation, but everything to do with that stupid dream. I still avoided looking at him. Instead, I kept my gaze fixed on Alec. In order not to say or do the wrong thing, I bit the inside of my cheek. "So, is it a game you want to play, then?" His voice was low and playful.

I exhaled a heavy sigh, kicked my heel into the side of my stallion, and sprinted to the head of our little group where Alec was walking, only looking at the smug smirk on Demetrius' face as I turned to speak with Alec.

"What are you doing, Zirena?" Alec sounded annoyed at my presence, and it stung a little.

"I am riding next to you." I played daft, and he gave me a look of incredulity.

"What are you doing speaking to me when clearly this is the perfect opportunity for an alone time with your matched?" I swallowed hard at that word and my gaze shot forward.

"I already had a moment with him right before riding up next to you," I said with a smile, but his expression told me he did not believe me yet again.

"It's understandable to be afraid. Being matched is an important and substantial change in a person's life.

It's very real and very permanent and I know Dem was an immature brat to you, but it steamed from his attraction."

Attraction? Is that what they call harassment and bullying these days? He pulled on my horse to stop and then looked up at me. "Dem has had feelings for you since we were children. He never knew what to do or say when he was near you. Your very scent got to him. You need to give him a chance, and I know you have seen the way he changed in these last few weeks."

"It still doesn't excuse his previous behavior, and if you were attracted to someone, would you go about harassing them and threatening to do the most inappropriate things to them?"

He was quiet for a moment before he answered.

"No, it does not."

We started again and there was silence for the next hour, with nothing but the distant sound of animals settling for their night and our day. Demetrius had switched with Alec at some point, but kept his distance from me, noting that I did not want to be near him. My thoughts drifted back to Rita and the way she was acting before she left for patrol.

"When I get back to Zia, we need to have a conversation." I noted the serious tone in her voice.

"What's wrong?" She was pacing, and I did not know what had her on edge. "Rita, tell me, please." She stopped her pacing, looked at me, and then embraced me with a tight hug. I wrapped my arms tight around her.

"I love you, Zia," she said as she pulled away from me and then just held my hands out in front. "You are like the daughter I never got the chance to have."

"Rita, you're scaring me." My heart was thrumming, and blood pumped in my ears at the difference in her demeanor. She was scared or nervous about something, and that was not a good thing to be before going on patrol.

"I will explain everything when I get back. I promise." She pressed a kiss to my brow and then left me standing in my room, puzzled.

I brushed it off to my upcoming birthday, or she knew about a potential match. But now I suspect it had more to do with what I changed into. Those thoughts of suspicion came back to me. If she tried to warn me and the lords found out, would they kill her and blame it on the mortals? There was no rational explanation for them wanting to keep this beast a secret from me unless—

A loud scream to the aft of me snapped me back to reality. I stopped my horse, grabbed the hilts of my daggers, and scanned the area.

"One of the guards is missing."

I heard Demetrius say as he came running to my right.

"Is it another pack?" I asked, trying to steady the rising panic in my voice. There was no howling, no pounding of paws. The forest is still like last time, just the whizzing of an arrow passing close enough to my ear. It nicked the side, sending a wince of pain through me.

"Get out of here, *now*," Demetrius yelled, and then slapped my horse on the rear to send it galloping into the night air.

We rode hard. I didn't dare look back or defy him. The last thing I wanted was to turn into a bloodthirsty killer again because I came so close to hurting them—

him. There were shouts and distant sounds of steel on steel. Who was out here to attack us? There was no civilization or community between the Caverns and the castle except for the wolves. It didn't sound like they were attacking; it sounded like other men attacking them. I pulled up on my reins, turned around, and then we raced right back to the fight.

If there were mortals stupid enough to cross over during their night and our day, I would not run. Not after what happened to Rita and so many others before her. I had a hunger for revenge and no one and nothing would stop me from sinking my teeth into it.

As soon as we were on the edge of the battle, I launched myself into the air, hit the ground with a thud, and rolled forward, slicing through the legs of a mortal who was fighting with Alec.

"What the hell?"

I smiled at him, got to my feet, and then charged forward, attacking the next one charging at us. He stopped at the sight of me. "You're a woman."

"No shit."

He stepped back, as though avoiding to fight me, a woman, but ended up right into Demetrius' blade. Blood seeped right where the blade went through his heart.

"He was mine."

Demetrius was angry with me, charged forward, and grabbed my wrist. "I told you to run."

"Get your hands off me before I slit your throat." He did not release me but motioned to Alec, who just killed the last mortal, then the unthinkable happened. "What are you doing?"

Rope was being tied around my wrist. Demetrius

pressed down on two pressure points, and I had no control. My fingers released my daggers until they tumbled and hit the ground. "Demetrius, you can't do this. Untie me now."

He ignored me. There was nothing but anger on his face as he pulled me to the trunk of a tree.

"Stop. You are going to regret this," I spat between clenched teeth.

I felt his hot breath on my neck as another rope wrapped my tied arms around the trunk of the tree, restrained so I could not turn around or break free. "You disobeyed me and now I punish you."

"Get your fucking hands off me." I refused to cry and did not show the fear that was rising. Any new feelings that I had developed for him quickly dissipated as if they never existed. I felt a sharp blade in between my tunic and skin, then the chilly breeze pricked at my bare back as Demetrius cut it in two. I stilled in place. There was nothing I could do, and I let my mind go blank, just like I did every time the lord punished me.

"I am to be your matched, Zirena. You will obey me and if you don't, this is to happen." I turned to look at him and then spit in his face.

"Fuck you." A burning slap across my face had a metallic taste develop in my mouth. Then I heard the whip, and the first slice of pain stunned my body with shock, but I did not let my weakened state show.

"There will be no more fighting, no more weapons." Each time he forbade me from doing something that I loved to do, he whipped me. Like he was trying to tear that piece of me out and turn me into some dainty submissive girl.

"No more training." Crack.

"No more leaving." Crack.

"No more tunics or breeches, only dresses." Crack.

"No more drawings or reading books." The wet warmness of my blood oozed out of my body, trickling down my spine.

"That's enough, Demetrius." It was Alec's voice, which surprised me.

"I will determine when she has had enough, and if you try to stop me again, you will—" I did not hear another word. The only sound I registered before the whip struck me was the gust of wind. Then there it was, the sound of twenty men running with their swords drawn. I waited for the fatal blow to me to land because I was utterly defenseless.

"Get the hell out of our territory before you all die."

I heard the snarl in his voice. He could not attack. There were not enough of them to defend against twenty mortals. "Is this what you do to your women? String them up and beat them until they bleed?"

That deep, husky voice sounded familiar to me, but I was fading in and out of consciousness. That told me my wounds were much deeper than expected. A warm, calloused hand brushes the hair out of my face and looks at me with pity.

"Get your hands off her," Alec hissed.

The mortal did not so much as acknowledge them. Did he not know that they were Immortals and could rip his throat out? Or if he did, he did not care, he just kept his deep green eyes on me as his hand gently cupped my cheek.

"Are you okay?"

I remained silent but nodded my weary head. Not

understanding if it was blood loss or just my imagination that a mortal man seemed to care about my well-being.

"You shouldn't interfere with our business." Demetrius hissed again. "That is my—"

"I don't give a fuck who this woman is to you. I will not stand by and let you beat her. Besides," —he paused and then stuck a finger in my mouth, checking my teeth.— "It seems to me this woman isn't an Immortal at all. She has no fangs, and she does not have those hideous black beads for eyes. And she bleeds."

"You do not know what you are talking about," Alec said. I sensed fear in his voice.

"I will ask you once and only once, girl, do you need help?"

I was still fading in and out, but he was gentle in his tone and touch that I nodded and let the darkness consume me once again.

Faint images of the canopy of trees and the midnight sky were the first things I saw as my eyes opened. The clanking of metal and screams of battle echoed in the backdrop. An arm was under my knees and the other wrapped around my shoulders as my head lay pressed into a firm chest. The scent was a lush of pine and cinnamon, mixed with blood. I saw the freshly shaved face of a brown-skinned man looking straight ahead. And then I faded into that darkness again. Words of whispers saying you are safe now before a sudden warmth washed over me followed by a bright light.

My eyes fluttered open slightly, and I saw it. My very first sunrise, or what I thought was one, and this must be a dream. I told myself there was no other explanation.

When I awoke, I noticed the ceiling above was made of stones, with dark wooden beams stretching across it. A smell of lavender and oil filled the room. I winced at the sharp pain in my back while sitting up, and then reality set in. The room I was in had three rows of beds lined with white sheets and pillows. Every few feet, there were desks lined with bandages and vials of liquids. There was a set of windows at the front and back walls of the room, but I was the only one inside.

I got to my feet, and the stone floor was cold to the touch. They had dressed me in a long white gown. I walked around, trying to figure out where I was and how I got here. It could be the Castle of Alvion. I mean, I've never been there before, so I wouldn't know what to expect. There was only one wooden door. After looking around for any sign of shoes or different clothes and not finding anything, I went straight for the door.

I peeked my head out and saw no one on either side of the hall. That was a good sign, I suppose. As I started to step out the door, my ears picked up distant voices and footsteps. Then they rounded the corner. Slinking back inside the room, I ran to my bed and immediately pretended to be asleep. The door creaked open, and distinct footsteps approached my bed. I was almost startled when a warm, calloused hand brushed my hair behind my ear. That familiar scent of lush and pine-filled my nose, and the flashes came back to me.

I am in the mortal world.

Part Two—The Soul Bonded

Chapter 10

I opened my eyes with the recollection that had just hit me.

"Good morning," he said. Then I sat up again, acting like I was in shock, which was partly true. "How are you feeling?"

"Where am I?"

"You're safe," he said. I looked down at where our thighs were touching on the bed. He must have seen my gaze because he got to his feet. Immediately, I got to mine on the other side of the bed.

"What happened? How did you get away with your life?" I genuinely wanted to know.

"Your Immortal friend was beating you to death and four Immortals can't take down a legion of men." His eyes met mine, not daring to look any lower than my face. I remembered him from the forest. That feeling of want and desire started pulsing in my veins, but I could not let it show, not here, not when he thought I was a mortal like him. My hands fisted so tight, my nails dug in so I could focus on the pain and not on the sensation coursing through every part of my body.

"Thank you for saving me," I said. He is just as beautiful as I remember. His face before was full of hair. Now, it was trimmed and cleaned as if it had never existed. But I would recognize that scent and those eyes anywhere. "Where am I?" I asked again.

"You are in the infirmary wing of Castle Camilion." He paused for a moment before continuing. "Are you not from here?"

"No." It was not a lie.

"How did you end up being a prisoner to those monsters across the border?" Ice hit my veins, and that desire quickly faded at what he called us. Not everyone was a monster, especially Rita, and they killed her.

"They took me when I was a babe. I've lived with them my entire life." Still not a lie, but if he prodded any further, I was not so sure I could lie to him. Even the thought tasted like death on my tongue.

"I'm sorry to hear that." He was. I saw the sincerity on his face and heard it in his voice. That ice quickly melted. "You are more than welcome to stay here for however long as you like."

"In the Infirmary?" I asked, and then he chuckled. It ignited that heat again. I have made no one laugh except Rita.

"No, there are bed chambers in the east wing of the castle. I will see that one is prepared for you, and I am going to have the tailor get you some clothes since you were a prisoner all your life."

"That's unnecessary. But thank you." He looked at me with disappointment. I preferred not to be locked inside a palace with people that would kill me if they knew what I truly was.

"You are not a prisoner. So, the choice is up to you, but I assume you do not want to travel in just a nightgown." I looked down at what I was wearing and then quickly covered my chest as I saw the peak of my nipples show. No wonder he averted his eyes.

Demetrius would not have cared. Bile crept up in my throat at the thought of him. Then the thought occurred to me whether he or Alec was alive. If I went back, what would happen to me?

"Did you kill them?" I asked.

"Yes, all except two of them. The one who was whipping you got away with the other one."

Shit. I cursed under my breath.

"Beg pardon?"

He heard me. Oh, gods. "I'm sorry."

"I've never heard a woman say that before." He smiled at me with intrigue. And my stomach did that stupid flutter thing again. Then it rumbled with hunger. "You must be famished. At least let me get you appropriate travel clothes and some food before you leave."

He was giving me a choice. Something that was being taken away from me back on the other side. I wanted to hug this man and thank him. Instead, I just asked, "Why are you being so nice to me?"

"What do you mean?"

"You don't know me, yet you had your healer tend to my wounds, and offered me a home with food and clothing." That curiosity crossed his face again.

"I can imagine kindness such as these being foreign to you, but my mother raised me to treat someone, man or woman, with the respect that I would want if the roles were reversed."

"Your mother sounds lovely."

"She was." Curiosity was quickly replaced by a pang of sadness in his eyes.

"I'm sorry for your loss."

"You have nothing to be sorry about. She died

many years ago." I wanted to ask if it was an Immortal that killed her, but that would be a very personal question. My stomach growled again. "Shall we feed you and bring you a change of clothes?"

"Yes, please, and thank you."

He smiled at me and led me out and into the hall.

"And some shoes." He glanced down at my bare feet. "What shall I call you?" he asked as we walked down a grand arched hall to the right of the infirmary.

There are marvelous ceiling-to-floor windows that saw out into a training yard of some sort. I glimpsed soldiers sparring with each other. The smell of the palace was a mix of many things I had never smelled before. Nothing awful or evil. We rounded a curve after about fifty feet, and grand paintings materialized, lining the walls. Each revealed their own story of the past. I stopped to admire the incredibly detailed and textured painting of a white mare grazing on a green plain. It was beautiful.

"Do you paint?"

That voice snapped me out of my head. "No." Revealing too much about myself was not an option. And then I remembered the question he asked me prior to that one. "My name is Zirena."

"Zirena," he said, as if he was asking if he pronounced it correctly. I nodded, impressed at how he got it on the first try. That was one thing about my name. No one ever pronounced it on the first try. Although, I had not really met anyone new since I was a child. Zi-re-nah was what I would say to anyone I met. "That is an exquisite name."

I smiled, my cheeks flaming with heat. "What shall I call you?"

"You may call me Dean." That confirmed it. As soon as he said his name, it confirmed that I had already met this man, indirectly of course, twice. That confirmed that he could not see me that day standing right in front of him. We held each other's gazes for a moment before the sound of approaching footsteps broke our silent interaction.

A man with brackish-colored hair, fair skin, and blue-gray eyes came upon us. He wore a crown of gold upon his head, along with a regal red robe draped over a black tunic and breeches. I at once curtsied or tried to. Something I was told to practice for when I met the queen but never wanted to. I was very off balance and nearly fell over when a firm hand caught my arm to balance me.

"Forgive me, Your Grace," I said.

"Dean, I believe we need to have a conversation...*now*."

I did not dare look at the king's face, but an icy stare directed right toward me.

"Right after I get our guest some new clothes and food."

I sucked in a sharp breath, waiting for the sound of a smack, but nothing came.

"Who are you, girl?" I heard the king ask.

Still not looking at him, my hands folding tightly in front of me, I posed the perfect position regardless of how I looked.

"My name is Zirena, sire."

"Look at me." Then I felt three gloved fingers upon my chin, willing my head up to eye level.

"Father," Dean warned, and then it hit me. Oh, gods. Dean was not just any mortal—he was a prince.

Heir to the throne of these barbaric men who slaughtered the one person I loved most in all the world. I suppressed that rising heat, begging the beast not to show itself. I watch a tan hand grip the king's wrist. "Let go of her. She has done nothing wrong."

The hand dropped from my chin, but Dean still had one firmly on my bicep.

"I shall speak to both of you in the Banquet Hall."

I tried to curtsey again, but Dean held me up high. As if to tell me not to. It made me wonder why? How was he able to defy his father, the king, with no punishment? The king and the two guards that were with him marched past us. We waited until their footsteps faded into the distance. Dean could no longer hear, but I could.

"I'm sorry about that."

I jerked my arm free of him and whirled on him.

"Don't you ever touch me again." I stormed off, not knowing where I was going. Not caring that I had just insulted a prince, who would hang me for it. I heard him running to catch up to me, and then he stepped right in front of me. "Get out of my way."

"You have no clue where you are going." He was about a foot taller than I was.

"I don't care. I will find my way out of here whether you like it or not."

"I can't understand the ordeal you must have gone through your entire life, but I will say this again—you are not my prisoner. You may leave as soon as you want, but since my father saw you, if you leave now, he will see you as a threat."

I choked out a laugh and then saw a smile that showed two dimples on either cheek. "You honestly think I am afraid of him? A Mor—" I stopped myself before I could continue saying that I wasn't afraid of some mortal king.

"Please accept my apologies for my father's behavior. I will ensure he never lays a finger on you again." He was so sincere, and I hated how much I believed him. "Are you really going to make a prince beg?"

I continued to stare at him, intrigued. Why would he treat me, a stranger, no doubt a peasant to him, like this? As if he had known me my entire life. I crossed my arms and continued to stare, wondering just how far he would go. Testing to see how much control I had over this situation. I smirked at him, and he just smiled right back at me. I felt a laugh building, but I swallowed it. "After the meeting with the king, I would like to leave."

I watched as his smile faded and a tight line formed on his lips as if he were upset at me for wanting to leave.

Chapter 11

The dress I decided upon was smooth and amazingly comfortable. It was an emerald green color, that was only slightly tight at my chest, and the rest flowed to the ground. I requested to not be forced into heels, but boots would be fine. That made Dean smile with intrigue even more. A maid helped me wash my matted hair and re-braid it, telling me how she wished she had such beautiful hair like mine. How was I able to grow it so long, and that it was the longest and most stunning hair she had ever seen or touched? I blushed at the compliments, and it made me wonder how anyone who would say such kind things can be barbaric.

I sat on a cushioned chair across from a brown hair girl with different colored eyes, one blue, and one green. She was dressed in a smaller gown similar to mine. They introduced her to me as Princess Antoinette. The feisty twelve-year-old little sister of Prince Dean. To my right sat Dean and the princess to my left, at the head of the table, the King. The feast laid out across the crimson-painted table was full of food I had never seen before in my life. I recognized the fish and venison, but not the assortment of fruit.

Fruit was a precious delicacy in the Caverns. Since the Coven and I needed to eat actual food to survive, it was not a priority. Meat was the major priority, but nonetheless, Rita got me a book all about how we had ancestors that would grow crops of all kinds of fruits and vegetables. Which made me ask her why the ancestors needed food, but they don't know? She simply answered that they grew the crops because they enjoyed it, not to survive. I asked her what they did with them, and she told me when the world was at peace, they would send it to the mortal realm to continue the peace between the lands.

The finery laid out before me was even more bewildering. A plate of pure gold with the Kingdom's royal crest emblazoned on it. Two golden clusters, appearing like leaves, crossed at the tip with a sword running through the middle. The utensils were just pure gold, and I could see my reflection looking back at me from the back of the spoon. Well, that is what the princess had called it. I was not used to eating with anything but my hands, but like Rita taught me, to watch, listen, and learn.

I did just that, as the princess used them to eat her food. "Is everything to your liking?" Dean's voice caught me by surprise.

"Yes. Thank you." I smiled at him, and then picked up the utensil called a fork. Watching how they held them—just like I gripped my charcoal to draw with—I poked the greens and took a bite, almost moaning at the flavor that burst in my mouth. It was nothing I had ever tasted before in my entire life. After this, I would ask just what those were called and eat them every day for the rest of my life. Then it dawned on me that I would not be staying here. I needed to get to Castle Alvion, meet with the queen and explain to her everything that happened. Prayed she would believe me.

"So, girl, Dean tells me you were a prisoner on the

other side." The King's question was laced with irritation.

I swallowed the bite I had just taken, swallowing the anger that was trying to seep through it.

"That's correct, Your Grace." I remembered my lessons well, or at least tried to.

"You were with them your entire life? How many years is that?" he asked through a mouth full of meat that suddenly ruined my appetite.

"Twenty-four, Your Grace," I said with a smile. Then I felt the warmth of Dean's leg pressing into mine as if to send another apology for how obviously rude his father was being toward me. I pushed back, trying to tell him it was not his fault, and that he was not responsible for his father's behavior. I am not sure if he got the message, but his leg moved, and the warmth was gone. Naturally, my hands fell to my lap, and I reached over to his hand, using the tablecloth to hide it, my heart beating erratically. I didn't know what I was doing or why. I just needed him to know it was not his fault.

My knuckles brushed his, and he did not flinch as I interlaced my fingers with his, our knuckles touching. I squeezed it once, then let go once he squeezed it back. It was as if we were speaking in a secret code that no one else in the world would understand except for us.

"Tell me, girl, are your parents alive?"

Dean's hand interlaces with mine again, this time palm to palm, telling me to use him as an anchor. I did not let the flush of heat show as I focused on the king and not the firm, warm hand holding mine. A small touch, not meant to be so intimate, but it was to me.

"No, my mother died during my birth, and I

assume the Immortals killed my father." Curiosity flashed in those blue-gray eyes of his.

"Why did they kidnap you? Why not just kill you like the rest of your family?" Another squeeze from Dean told me it was okay. His touch helped to soothe me.

"They told me I was used as an experiment. That once I reached my twenty-fifth year of life, I would be matched with one of their own."

The king snorted in disgust.

"They were grooming you for breeding. Typical of those disgusting monsters." Another gentle squeeze from Dean. "Well, you are here now. Safe from them, what are you to do?" he asked, and I didn't really have an answer because I was planning on going back.

"I…" I hesitated and Dean answered for me.

"I will give her sanctuary until she can find a job and lodging of her own."

"And who, pray tell, will pay for her food and clothing?" The king's eyes, like icy daggers toward his son, had a fire burning in me. An unnatural reaction to a man I just met.

"I will, Father." Dean was stern and held his gaze on his Father. There was tension building, and I could scent the rise in testosterone. It was very amusing.

"If I may, Your Grace, I would like to earn my keep." Better to keep the damsel in distress façade up while I can. The king and Dean did not dare look at me as they continued their silent debate.

"I think that is unnecessary, Zirena." It was Dean who answered. Gods, no one had ever defended me as he has in the past twenty-four hours. I really wanted to hug him tight and thank him for defending me, but I released my grip from his hand and placed it, daringly, upon his thigh, squeezing it gently, causing him to jerk slightly.

"I am inclined to allow this, but first I have terms of my own." I saw Dean's eyes glare with distrust at his father. And then the king's gaze went straight to me. "You may not leave the castle grounds. You will work in the kitchens as a servant girl, and you will move to quarters appropriate for a woman of your status. My healer will check to see if your maidenhood is indeed intact. Once I receive word that you are still a maiden, you will move about this castle. If you think for one second you can step out of these walls without my knowing, it would be a foolish mistake." He paused for a moment, sipping wine from his goblet.

"Dean may not interact with you in any familiar way. You will address him as Your Highness, never look at his face, and will not become friends. You and your history with the scum beyond the wall, as pitiful as your story sounds, I do not trust you. My son has eyes for a young woman with a bountiful breast, but that does not mean I will treat you any better than the scum of my kingdom." I am seething mad now and felt my fangs elongating, ready to launch myself onto him, damning the consequences, but I did not need to.

Dean was on his feet in mere seconds, hand on his hilt, defending my honor yet again. "You are the king, and you are my father, but you have no right to treat her in such a disrespectful manner. If Mother were alive, she would not treat Zirena as poorly as you are right now. And because you are my father, your head is still on your shoulders." Dean turned to me and extended a hand, which I obliged, and without another word, we stormed out.

****

"Dean," I said, but he was still pulling me hard behind him.

"Stop." I stood my ground and jerked my hand away from him. I could smell the anger wafting off his skin. How can one man be so angry with his father for speaking to me in such a manner? Someone he did not know at all.

"I'm so sorry for what my father said. He is…" He growled and turned toward me. "I don't want you to believe one word he said. If I have anything to say about it, you can walk right out of the palace gates. Hell, I will walk with you." Surprise hit me as I gazed at him. Why would this man risk prison and death for me? There must be more to his story. His anger is not natural.

"No." I was stern with him, and he gave me an inquiry look. We stared at one another, me not breaking my cool stare, and him with dark brows furrowed in confusion. His scent was a mix of lush spice and arousal. It caused my cheeks to flame before I broke the stare. "I will do as your father commands because you don't know me and neither does he. He has every right to suspect me because of the circumstances of my life."

His shoulders lifted, and he let out a sigh of defeat. "There is something intriguing about you."

I looked down before he could see the smile that was trying to show, and then I brushed past him toward my quarters. Getting a waft of that arousal increasing as our arms slightly brushed, I could use his attraction toward me as an advantage. Manipulate him into helping me slaughter the king and everyone else responsible for Rita and countless other lives. Then the question of what to do, when, and how tugged at me.

Sure, Demetrius' behavior was disgusting, and I was going to slit his throat the next time we met. Alec too. I am sure once the queen gets word of what happened, he will try to make it sound as if I betrayed them, so by taking down Camilion and hand delivering the Mortal Prince's and the king's heads, would show the queen that whatever story Demetrius had concocted was wrong. Then I would tell her of what that sadistic asshole did to me and pray to the gods she would not let the Matching Ceremony go forward. Sex dream or not, there was no way in hell they would ever let that vile creature touch me again.

I lay down on the edge of the bed, legs spread wide, revealing my exposed sex to the female healer. This was the first time anyone—but me—was going to touch it. I did not think it would be a woman. The healer was wearing a simple white dress, down to the floor, a white head cap that connected to the color of the dress. The only exposed skin was her wrinkled, fair-skinned face and freezing hands.

"Are you a maiden?" she asked, her voice pitchy.

"Yes, madam." I was not sure how to address her, so I remembered what Rita had taught mc about manners and respect. If they do not have a title or you do not know it yet, call them madam or sir.

"Then I should tell you to brace for the pain that is about to happen, and I apologize for it." She held up a metal device shaped like a cone. My heart pounded. *Oh, gods, she is not putting that in me, is she?* "This is called a speculum. There is a magnifying glass at both ends that allows me to see your entire anatomy. If you have not been with a man before, I will see a small sack of blood untouched. Even without touching it, I will be gentle, but it will hurt a bit. I have doused it with lavender and oil." I was nearly shaking. This feels like a violation. I rarely scare easily but this... Utter humiliation.

"Isn't there another way?" I asked, my voice shaking.

"The only other way is for you to be bedded. The bloody show of a maiden occurs—"

"I know." I hated the trembling in my voice. The old woman's face was not angry or surprised at my outburst but expressed pity.

"What will it be, girl?" she asked softly.

"Just do it, for the love of the gods."

Then she told me to take a deep breath in. The hard metal slowly eases into me. There was pain, a burning-like sensation, but she was terribly slow with each wince of pain.

"Almost done, girl. Just breathe through it." Doesn't the sheer fear and pain on my face tell this woman all she needs to know? Gods, is this my punishment? Then she eased it out of me, and the pressure and tightening eased. "I'm sorry, dear girl. I will report to the king that your maidenhood is indeed intact."

I remained on the bed with my eyes closed as I heard her packing up her tools. She let out a sigh before walking and then stopped right before opening the door. "It won't be like that."

I sat up and stared at her, my brows furrowed. She walked toward me, pressed a gentle hand on my cheek, and said, "When you share a bed for the first time, it won't be like that."

"What will it be like?" I was very curious because I really was not sure I ever wanted to have sex with anyone after that.

"It will still hurt slightly, but if the man does his job correctly, pleasure and passion will mask the pain. I have only ever had one man in my life—my dear late husband." She smiled and released my cheek. "Aron was a wonderful husband. On our wedding night, I was just as terrified as you were. He did not push, did not rush. He even told me we did not have to and could just act like it happened until I was ready. But of course, I called him a fool because healers always check the wife to give the official seal that the marriage was consummated."

"Did you not know your husband before?"

"No. The Matchmaker chose us because my father needed money and Aron wanted to be rid of his one and only child. He will pay any price so long as Aron was married."

"I'm sorry." The woman was being honest, and I truly felt sorry for her.

"Don't be. Aron and I grew to love each other deeply. The Matchmaker knows precisely what she is doing. It is a blessing from Hena, the Goddess of fertility and love. Have you been to a Matchmaker yet?"

"That's not how the other side does things." I dropped my gaze, afraid of judgment from this exceedingly kind, strange lady that was now familiar because she had seen my sex and been the first person to insert something inside of me. The thought, and not-so-distant memory of that thing inside me, sent a shiver down my spine.

"Do not fear, girl. You will get no judgment from me. If you would like, if the king permitted, I could set up a meeting with the Royal Matchmaker."

"That won't be necessary, but thank you." The woman patted me on the shoulder and then made her way out of the bed chambers. But just before the door closed all the way, a voice sounded from the hall.

"Zirena, may I come in?" This man just does not know when to leave someone alone.

"Yes." I made sure the skirt of my dress was back down. Still very naked underneath. When he walked in, my breath caught with that rush of his scent hitting me. My heart began thrumming again, skin and core heating with lust and desire. My vision fixated on the vein on his neck, egging me toward it. Taste me. Drink me. Kiss me.

"Are you all right?" His question lifted me out of my daze.

"Yes."

He scooted a chair to sit in front of me. Leaning over with his elbows resting on his knees, that shaggy brown hair fell slightly forward, and my fingers tingled with the urge to touch it. He seemed nervous. I took a deep breath in, smelling the powerful scent of him. His normal one: spices, arousal, and nerves.

"Is there something I can help you with?"

He dragged a hand across the back of his neck before speaking. "Are you okay? Did she hurt you?" I heard myself giggle because he looked so worried. "Well, you're laughing, so that's good."

"Your healer has a gentle touch."

He seemed like he desperately wanted to ask me

something else. Something that had him on the edge of his seat.

"I'm a virgin, Dean."

I cupped my mouth, not sure why I just blurted such an inappropriate and clearly unnecessary statement. Right away, the tension in his shoulders eased as if my confession brought him relief. I scooted further off my bed until our knees brushed together. It was clear Dean wanted me. His eyes and scent were full of lust, and I could use that to my advantage.

Until he was a dog on my chain, I could give him a little taste.

"I should leave. I'm sorry." He shot up to his feet, but so did I. Closing the small distance between us, the tips of my breasts slightly brushed against his chest. He looked down at me, and I could smell his lust growing even more.

"I never properly thanked you for saving my life," I said as I ran one singular finger down his jawline, watching as a shudder ran through his body. That made me feel powerful. He was hardening against me. He wanted me so badly it was killing him to not just take me.

"That won't be necessary." He could not hear the nerves in his voice, but I could. I wanted to see if this man had any honor, so I took one of his hands and brushed my lips gently across it. Cupping his cheek, I raised to my tiptoes, his breath hot on my lips, and he wanted to kiss me, but I turned his head, kissing his cheek, then his ear, nipping it slightly, and then his neck. He placed his hands on my hips. I smiled into his neck.

Then his lips brushed mine because I had given

him the permission he needed. His kiss on my neck sent a wave of heat rushing through me, and my sex throbbed and ached. Oh, gods. No one has ever kissed my neck, and it felt good. Far better than that stupid dream. He pulled me into him tighter and he broke away from my neck. His eyes are full of curiosity and lust. "Do you want this?" he asked. His breath was heavy.

I did not answer with words. I grabbed the back of his head and pulled him onto me and the bed. His hair was silky and smooth, and he ground into me, sending a moan to escape my lips. I reached down to feel him. He shuttered at my touch. It was not even skin-to-skin, so I thought about what it would be like with no clothes on. He kissed my neck again, his hands exploring my body. My legs wrapped around his waist, and he sat up on his hunches bringing me with him. Our breathing was ragged and urgent, and he stared at me with those deep-sea eyes with wonder and respect.

This was better than any dream because this was real. Even though I wanted to tell myself that I was pretending, it was a lie. My eyes zoomed in on that vein in his neck, my ears tuning into the pounding of his heart rate, and the blood flowing. I felt their presence after my mouth watered with hunger. My fangs elongated, and I could not stop them. The sexual tension between us was too much. I needed to taste him to know what it was like to have that length inside of me. I brushed my mouth on his neck, licking, teasing as his hands bunched up the skirt of my gown, hand brushing up my thigh, but before he could feel me, I jerked away.

I was on the back wall in an instant and he

remained sitting on the bed, confused at what happened and how I got there so fast. I looked away, silently commanding my fangs to retract, but I knew they would not. Not until everything would calm down. Not until he was gone. "Get out."

"Zirena." I heard the worry and disappointment in his voice, and it hurt me.

"Dean, I need to go to bed. I'm not ready." It was a lie. I was ready despite the pain I felt before he walked into this room. What the Healer told me about what it was like to be with a man was something that sparked my interest.

I heard him get off the bed, walk to my door, open it, and then said, "I'm sorry if I hurt you."

The door slammed, startling me, and tears swelled in my eyes. I took it too far too soon. Why do I want him so badly? He is the enemy. He is a mortal. I should not care if I drain him dry. I have wanted nothing so badly, but if I lose control and kill him too soon, it will get me killed. I know I can take this entire castle by force if I need to, but I need to be smarter. I need to control whatever this is that I have for him. I need to run. Running has always helped me clear my mind, but it was forbidden to leave the grounds. But the moon is about to be high in the sky, and that means all the mortals will soon be asleep. Except for those on watch, which I can slip past all of them in a blink of an eye.

I removed the flimsy dress, washed the oil and lavender from my sex, dressed in a tunic and breeches, and slipped out the window. The ledge was about a foot wide, but I trained to walk on slim ledges like this since I could walk. After falling two hundred times, bleeding, and breaking a few bones, I finally got the hang of it.

There were no guards that would see or hear me if I was careful enough. The black cloak I wore helped to hide me in the midnight sky. Pulling myself up onto the stone roof of the palace, I ran, jumping into the air, until I landed twenty feet from the palace walls, and then took off.

The wind felt great through my hair, grass between my bare toes with each touch of my feet, and the feel of freedom with each stride. I could keep running and not stop until I reached Castle Alvion. I could keep running and never stop until I reach a new kingdom. They taught me about the possibility of three mortal kings. Unsure of what their names are and where we found them, but they would not be too far.

The chiming of bells rang in my ears, halting me in my tracks, and echoing in the distance. Oh, gods, do they know I ran? I made my way back and fast before they discovered I was gone. So, I ran, jumped, and climbed. Hanging on that ledge, I heard a loud banging and the sound of keys at my door. I quickened my pace, jumped into my window, and went straight to my bed. My door burst open, and I acted like I was awake.

"What in the gods is going on?" I yelled. Dean and three guards barged into my room. There were several awkward exchanges of glances between Dean and myself.

"We are under attack," he stated, and I felt relief flood over me. They did not know who or what I am, and that was a good thing.

"And did you think the intruders were in my chambers? Disrupting my much-needed sleep?" I scowled at them, throwing the blankets off me, revealing the silk nightgown I had thrown on after tossing my running clothes aside. An advantage of being half-immortal was the blessed speed. Although the Immortals were faster than I was at everything, I was faster than these mortals were. I walked up to the four of them, noting that the chilly breeze blowing through my window had the peaks of my nipples hard and this nightgown was not hiding anything.

"Zirena," Dean started, and the three guards walked out into the hall, two remaining posted right outside my door. The third one waited for Dean. I walked up to Dean, closing the distance.

"What do you want, Dean?" He sighed, his gaze drifting from my face down the length of my body and slowly coming back up. "Do you see something you like?"

"What game are you playing?" he asked. Frustration was evident in his tone, despite the obvious scent of lust wafting from him. I crossed my arms across my chest and turned around. Whenever he was around, I couldn't think. I forced myself to try and regain some type of composure. All I wanted was the hunger for him and his blood. His cock inside of me and his blood in my mouth. My emotions were too confusing, the feelings far too strong, and thank the damn gods that the door was open, and those three guards were outside or else I would pounce on him and let him take me right here, right now.

"Dean, I've never kissed or touched. Intimacy with anyone, until the Matching Ceremony, is forbidden to me. I have never had feelings or any attraction to anyone before now." I paused, my back still to him, but I could feel him inches from my back. His breathing skyrocketed. "I thought Demetrius had changed, and I started, or I thought I felt something other than disgust for him. But it was all an illusion or the inevitability of the Matching Ceremony." I let out a rapid breath as I felt him come closer, his breath hot on my neck, sending waves of arousal through me.

"I was always in control of everything. My emotions and actions. I was the perfect soldier, despite the Immortals. Until I am around you." His hands touched my shoulders, and I flinched. "You don't know me, Dean, and if you were smart, you would execute me where I stand. I am a danger to you and your people."

Damn it. Why am I telling him all this? He said we were under attack. Could Demetrius have found me? What would he do? This will not help with my plan, although there really is not much of a plan to start with. I stepped out of his grasp, but he pulled me into him, wrapping his arms around me in a loving embrace. Something yet again new to me. I could easily get away from him if I wanted to. But that was *if* I wanted to.

"Zirena," he whispered in my ear. "I know we are strangers, but when I am near you, I am pulled to you. I can't explain it. When I am away from you, I need to be near you. And when you kissed me? I thought and prayed it would never end, but then you jumped out of my arms and told me to get out. My heart hurt and I thought it was because I hurt you."

A tear trickled down my right eye.

"Dean, this isn't real. The only logical explanation is some sort of hero complex and damsel in distress. You saved me from death and so I am attracted to you. And you are to me. But I cannot let this go further than it has. Your father would disapprove, and you are a prince. You are duty-bound to marry a noblewoman or princess. If I let you into my bed, it will damn us both." Everything was quiet except our breathing, the guards' breathing, and the heartbeats between all of us.

"I don't care." He gripped the back of my neck tightly, turning me toward him, and kissing me deeply. His tongue scraped against the roof of my mouth and my teeth.

A faint thought surged through my head. If I lose control, my fangs will show, and I may kill him. I pulled away from him and was against the wall, hyperventilating.

"How do you keep getting away from me so fast?"

I did not dare answer him. He stalked toward me like a predator toward its prey. I could see the outline of his manhood hardening against his tight breeches, and it sent a wave of heat between my thighs.

"Do you like what you see?" His voice sounded sultry.

"Dean."

He pressed a finger to my mouth.

"Do you want me? Do you want this?" I did, and I really wanted to tell him yes and let him take me right up against this wall.

"We can't, and tomorrow I need to leave."

"I will respect your wishes, Zirena. And I know that this frightens you. But I assure you of one thing."

"What's that?"

"That this is more than physical attraction."

"How could you possibly know? Because you have had many women?" He stepped away from me. The tension between us lessened. "Your people need you. If your palace is under attack."

95

"Goodnight, Zirena."

I heard the pain of my words in his voice. I hurt him again. This man who wants me is kind to me but does not know what a veritable monster I am. The one that has fangs, horns, talons, and wings. I know this is more than physical, but, gods, I cannot be soul bound to a mortal. It is not right. The anger rising in me was so much that I slid to the floor, crying. I cannot do this anymore. I needed answers.

Lucan, if you can hear my prayers, you bastard, answer me.

Chapter 12

"It isn't right to yell at a god girl." I opened my eyes. A tall man with black hair and golden eyes was standing right in front of me. I jumped and reached for my blade. "You can't kill a god girl and you aren't in any danger."

"Who are you?" My entire body itched with unease as I looked frantically at my closed door.

"Don't worry, your precious guards can't hear a word we are saying. I put a shield around this room even if they check on you. They will see you soundly sleeping in that bed." This cannot be real. "I am very real, Zirena."

"Get out of my head."

"If they taught you like I instructed those damned fools, I wouldn't be able to get in your head, you wouldn't lose control of yourself, and you wouldn't be nearly biting the prince's head off because your lust for him is far too great."

"Lucan?" I guessed, and he gave me a pitiful bow before speaking.

"At your service."

"What are you doing here?"

"You called, and I answered."

"I thought you were asleep. The lords said—"

"Listen to me, Zirena. Those idiots do not know what they are saying."

"Answer my questions."

He smiled at me, showing all white teeth and four fangs, not just two.

"Let us drink because I have heard you screaming at me for months. You don't know how loud you are and it's annoying." Two wine glasses and a pitcher appeared on the wooden table in the center of the room. He motioned to the chair across from him as he sat down and drank. The liquid was a crimson color, and I sniffed it. "It isn't blood, if you are wondering. Although, I expect once you get your first taste, you won't be able to stop."

"I have maintained control," I said as I sipped the bitter wine.

"Tell me, girl, how have you been able to resist sinking your teeth down on him? Or resisting to bed him?"

I rubbed my sweaty hands on the skirt of my lap. "That's a personal question."

"I mean, I can guess, and I will be right, but I just need to hear it, to ease my curiosity." I rolled my eyes. Lucan was not what I expected a god to look like. He appeared just like a mortal man with tanned skin, a muscled body, and black shaggy hair. The only difference was those sharpened four canines, pointed ears, and golden eyes.

"I don't know why or how I have been able to stop myself. I almost didn't." I let out a ragged breath because that was not the answer he wanted. "When I first saw him, in the forest outside your temple, I almost pounced on him for being a mortal in our lands. But there was something else. A feeling that told me it was not right, and that I did not just want to taste his blood, but I wanted him to be mine. It happened again after that and then I kissed him." I took a sip and Lucan was listening intently.

"I wanted to seduce him, but after we collided, everything changed. I could not stand the thought of betraying him, and all I wanted to do was let him take me until I could not breathe. Something is wrong with me. Full of lust for a mortal that if he knew who I was, what I was, he would kill me. His father has already threatened to." I took another sip, waiting for him to interject.

"I am sure you are aware of what I changed into when the pack of wolves attacked us?" He nodded and waved for me to continue. "Please tell me what is wrong with me? Don't give me a bullshit answer. I do not care whether you are a god. The one that created me. This also brings another question. Why?"

He emptied his chalice and began.

"I should've known those lords would disobey me."

"What—"

He put a hand up to silence me.

"It's my turn to speak, girl. Don't be rude."

I sipped my wine and motioned for him to continue. It was weird being around him. He was so familiar to me, like I had known him for years. It could be because his blood runs through my veins or it could be because he is my god. Regardless, I waited for answers.

"Before I blessed your mother with you, I told those idiots that you had to be trained to become the next Queen of Alvion. That you would need to master your powers and learn to be the bridge that would bring peace between the two realms. I created you to be half of me and half mortal. I did not mean you to be soul bound to anyone, but my dear sweet sister, your Auntie Hena, likes to meddle with people." He took another sip of his wine, continuing to stare at me.

"The lords clearly disregarded everything I ordered them to do with you except your warrior training, which I am extremely impressed with. And when your dear guardian Rita got a vision from me, she knew the truth." He paused, and I wanted to ask what it was. "Rita found out that the lords and the Coven were planning to drain the blood from you to become the Elite. When the lords found out, she knew they would kill her and five others, passing it off as an attack from the other side." My blood was boiling, swallowing back ire.

"Mind your temper, girl." He looked at me and I let out a breath I did not realize I was holding. "After you went into those Caverns, those witches put a shield around you and none of us gods could see you until you were gone. Your dear Uncle Remus, God of War, sent the wolf pack against the caravan you were traveling with to free you. None of us knew you would turn into a Skita." My brows wrinkled in confusion, and he answered my unspoken question. "A Skita, dear girl, is a demi-god. You not only have my powers but the powers of many other gods.

"You can fly, have super strength and speed. You have all the powers of an Immortal and that of the gods. They told so many lies that blood will taint you, but they were starving you because they were suppressing your powers. Once you drink, you will be unstoppable, and that is what they feared." He sipped again. "Did I answer everything, my dear?"

I ran through everything he said, but I still wanted to know more. And it all rushed out of me like vomit. "Are you my father? How can I control my powers? What will happen if I let my desires and lust fold?"

"Slow down, Zirena. I am like a father, but I did not bed your mother. She was a virgin. You will need time, practice, and a mentor to help you. And as far as your desires for the prince, it will happen eventually. That is a natural emotion when you find the one your soul is matched with. But until you control your bloodlust, the risk of killing him is too high."

There was silence between us, and I had a mixture of emotions running through me. Everything was making sense to me and now I wanted vengeance.

"Who, when, and where do I start my training?"

He gave me a wicked yet proud smile.

"Not that simple. There is no one alive that could help you, only a god can help you."

"So, train me."

He let out a laugh, but I held my gaze on him, showing him just how serious I was.

"If I agree to train you, you must listen to everything I say. I know what an obedient warrior you are. When I tell you to back off from your prince, you cannot argue with me. The first time you drink, it has to be from him."

"No, I can't."

"He is soul bound to you. His blood will be the only one that will give you the most strength and use of your powers. I will ensure you do not kill the boy, and will teach you how to erase his memory."

"I can't do that to him or anyone. They need to be

willing, and I don't think telling the prince everything will have him pressing my mouth to his neck ever again."

"I hear your concerns, and they are valid. But I need you to understand that if your first blood is not his, then your bond with him will weaken. I know they scared you, to tell him the truth, but his heart is growing for you every time he is near you. Your dear auntie can reassure you if need be."

"So, my options are to train to become all-power, drink from Dean, or train and don't drink, and then not get justice for everything those vile monsters have done?"

"Well, when you put it like that, you make it sound like you are choosing between life and death."

"Because I am. Dean will never agree with any of this."

"I can help with that."

"How?"

"Joel is the god of wisdom and truth. Once you have your heart-to-heart with your dear prince, Joel will be there, and Dean will tell you the truth from his heart. If it goes south, I will erase his memory and you will then need to choose." He paused, rose to his feet, and stretched with an obnoxiously loud yawn. "I will let you think on it and when you decide, just call out my name."

"I'll do it." Lucan gave me a wicked smile. "But I have conditions." I paused, waiting for him to say something sly.

"Well?" he asked and waved me on.

"If I train, it needs to be without blood." He went to interrupt me, but I continued, forcing him to remain quiet while I finished. "I never asked to be created like this. I never wanted to drink mortal blood to survive. It is not right and if everything you are saying is true, then the Immortals are the evil of this world. I do not want to be like them, no matter whose blood runs through my veins. I will fight to end the Immortals because you should have never created them. And you never should've created me." I waited for a reprimand, but Lucan just calmly looked at me.

"I need to have something for control, so I don't lose myself around him. I do not want to drink or bring him into my bed just because of a soul bond. It needs to be real and wanted. If you have something to subdue our desires for one another, then oblige, or else I will not train, and I will slit my throat." I saw him wince at that comment and he pondered my words. Walking over to me, he placed a hand on my cheek. I was expecting it to be cold, but it was warm.

"I know you are frightened, my child, but I will agree to your conditions. But I must warn you, even if you master all your powers, you will be useless against the Immortals. You're a Skita, the first and only since the beginning of creation." His voice was soft like I imagined my father to be. He pressed a kiss to my brow and then backed away from me before speaking again.

"When you are ready to taste, I will be with you, but be aware that if it is anyone other than your matched, you will turn into the very creatures you are now set on destroying."

"I know."

"Are we in agreement, my child?" I nodded. "Hold out your right arm." I did as I was told, and he gripped my wrist. Gently. "This may hurt."

A searing heat scorched across my skin as silver tendrils of ink raced up my arm to my right shoulder. "Gods," I swore, and he chuckled, and then the pain was gone.

"What did you do to me?" I asked, running a finger over my now tattooed arm.

"That is Marie." He named it. As if it were alive. And then the ink moved and floated off my skin and formed a physical shape of a feline. Silver fur glistened in the firelight and deep blue eyes looked back at me. A long tail curled around itself.

"Hello, Zirena." It spoke.

"Marie is a familiar. She will be the one to train you."

"A cat?" This was so incredible I couldn't stop myself from blurting it out. Marie's tail twitched in the most elegant way, and I could sense her wanting to claw my face for the insult I made toward her. Lucan pet Marie and I heard a purr of approval come from the feline.

"I take it you know little about familiars, so I will briefly explain. These magical creatures appear as common pets, but underneath all that beautiful fur is a genuine force of nature. Marie is not just a house cat, especially when her charge is threatened. She shifts into her true form. They are very loyal no matter if their charge is good or evil. Only the gods can bless someone to have one. Since I and your aunts and uncles cannot always be with you, we have granted you a familiar. I think with time, you two will grow to love and respect each other and, with that, your bond will become stronger. I urge you, my darling Zirena, to listen and learn from her. Because there is no other choice than this if you don't want to kill your precious human prince."

Chapter 13

It had been a month since I last saw or heard from Dean, except for the healer, who I later learned was called Maggie. She told me the night of the attack, the prince was sent off with a squadron of guards to fend off the castle. During that time, I had awkward meals with the king and princess. Marie was visible only to me, as well as my tattoo. She didn't enjoy staying on my skin, so she would just perch on my shoulder or lie on my lap. Sleeping, licking, purring when I pet her and giving me lessons on how to protect my mind.

"Your mind is your strongest weapon," she whispered in my ear. Her whiskers tickle me and I squirm slightly backward. "Once you can block out everyone from entering it, then you will not be vulnerable up there."

"Besides the gods, who has that kind of magic?" I asked as I practiced summoning a wall around myself and then got my answer as I felt invisible claws scratching inside of my head.

"Block me, girl," she hissed and although I have been practicing for over a week, it was still difficult to keep my wall for an extended period. "If you would just get over this pitiful angst about blood, you wouldn't struggle so much."

"Well, I don't want to survive on it," I hissed back at her, and then my walls came crumbling down, but before she could sink those invisible claws into me, she retracted. Sweat trickled down my body and my head throbbed. It was the most exhausting thing she had ever done.

"Zia." Marie found out my nickname the first day we started training. She could get into my mind and see my entire life laid out before her. She asked permission to use it, knowing what that name meant to me, and I granted it. Partly because Rita would not want it to disappear just because she was dead, and partly because I missed hearing it. "Any familiar, gods blessed, or god can get into minds and control people. Other magical beasts have the ability and if they get into your mind, they can flip your switch, and you will no longer be you until they say so."

"Is there no other way without blood? I mean, for me to get stronger?" Marie lowered her head and shook it from side to side. "What do I do?"

"Would you like me to be blunt?"

"Always," I said as I smiled at her.

"The prince is soul bound to you, always has been since before you both took your first breath. Hena does not always bless individuals like that. You two have a connection that, if strengthened, would make you both unstoppable. If you drink from him, you will stop. I will stop you. And when he drinks from you…" She paused as I shot her a questioning glance because Lucan never mentioned that before.

"It is necessary for a mortal to do so if they are soul bound with an Immortal or Skita, in your case. It signifies that you will not, and he will not accept blood from anyone else for life or death. The last part of the consummation of the two is sacred."

"If I meet my dear aunt, remind me to punch her in the gut for making this so damn hard." Marie let out a laugh and then so did I. It was getting comfortable being around her because she reminded me a lot of Rita. With her challenging yet calm demeanor. She pushes my limits, and I have grown fond of it over the past couple of weeks. Especially when my mind kept replaying the images of Dean's lips on me. Wondering and praying I did not screw this up entirely. Then Lucan sent a message to Marie to stop praying so loud about the prince. That I barely knew what it is to be Soul Bonded.

The sounds of bells broke me out of my thoughts. I rushed toward the window, which was foolish because all I could see was the courtyard and not the front gates of the palace. Rushing out of the room, Marie slung back into my arm, and I asked the guard what was going on.

"The Prince has returned." My heart beat so fast with anticipation. "If you want to see him, I suggest going to the throne room. It is a protocol for the king to announce the prince's return to the rest of the council."

"Thank you, Jorah."

Chapter 14

"He was the one leading the attack," Dean said as I entered the crowded throne hall. Royal dignitaries dressed in various regal attire were lined against the edge of a long rug.

Everyone appeared to be gawking at the prince and his battered company standing in the center front of the room. From behind, I could not see any visible injuries on Dean, but I smelled blood and cinnamon and my heart fluttered with worry. The prisoner was on his knees with his wrists bound by iron chains behind his back, connecting to a steel collar slightly hidden underneath a black cloth.

The scent wafting from the prisoner seemed familiar to me, almost reminding me of home.

"How many men did we lose this time?"

"Twenty, sire," Dean solemnly answered. I watched as the king got to his feet, charging toward his son.

"Retract your fangs, Zirena," Marie frantically whispered into my ear. Lifting my hand to cup my mouth, I tried to hide the sharpened canines but felt resistance.

"They won't budge," I whispered back. Marie let out a hiss.

"You need to leave before they find out what you truly are." She was right, but I can't get them to retract.

Something had triggered them, but what?

"It will be on you to tell those wives that they are now widows because of your inept ability to lead a regiment of men. You will apologize to the fatherless children, and you will do it without protest. Do you understand me, boy?" The way he was yelling at Dean was not helping with the burning anger coursing through my veins. I readied to pounce and rip that evil man apart.

Taking a step toward them, a soft touch of a furred paw on my right cheek stopped me.

"Zirena, look at me," Marie said in a soothing tone. "Look at me before you do something stupid and kill us both."

Turning my gaze to my feline friend, I saw the red clouding my gaze. The faint pounding of heartbeats filled my ears. All were calm except for the king's.

"Zirena, you need to get out of here *now*." Marie was patting my face, trying to get me to snap out of the blood rage. That is what Marie warned me about during our first week together. The longer I go without it, the closer I am to losing control.

If that happens, the beast will take over and no one will stop me, except the gods. Before I turned to leave, the king dismissed everyone. Dean turned and our eyes locked. My heart stopped when I saw the cut trailing across his right cheek. The bruises formed around his thick neck told me just how close he came to dying.

The cloud of red receded as he approached me. His hands were clasped behind his back, shoulders, and chest taut as he strode past me, stopping right as our shoulders brushed each other. I turned to look at him. Our eyes locked, a silent conversation of understanding.

"Dean," I began, but words failed me. My gaze wandered to the purple marks around his neck.

"Don't worry, Zirena. You should've seen the other guy." He spoke with a charming smile that roused a chuckle out of me. Something I have not done in a while and greatly missed.

"Do it again," he said. I did not understand what he meant at first. "That is the first time I have seen you smile since I met you."

"Considering the fact that we only met a little over a month ago, I'd say that isn't difficult to believe." I heard purring in my ear, telling me just how much Marie approved of Dean.

"I guess it also didn't help that I was gone for a month." He smiled as he spoke, brushing a dirty hand through his shaggy brown hair. I enjoyed watching the way he got nervous around me.

"You stink," I said at last while scrunching up my nose. The urge to suppress the stench tickling my nostrils failed me.

"A month in the woods will do that to a man with limited resources."

"I'm glad you are back," I said. His smile faded slightly. "I know we left things unsaid before—"

"Nothing needs to be said, Zirena. I will see you later." He gave me a swift bow before sauntering out of the throne hall, leaving the unspoken conversation still unspoken.

Walking toward my quarters, Marie perched on my shoulder, un-linking herself from my arm.

"That was slightly awkward."

"I have ruined things." Starting with her paw, Marie bathed herself while I continued to walk to my room.

"Don't tell me you are going to cry about a lost love. That would be absolutely dreadful." She purred.

"I will not cry, but this causes problems with the plan."

"What plan is that?" I gave her a skeptical glance. "The one about you becoming your true self and needing Dean's blood to do it, but instead of just taking it by force, you want him to give it up willingly?"

"Yes," I snapped.

"Don't get snappy with me, girl. I am only here to help you. Just because your lover boy doesn't want to talk about your feelings, that doesn't mean the feelings he felt for you just disappeared."

"It makes little sense," I said as I opened my door, closed it, and then plopped down on my bed as Marie comfortably perched on the edge of it. "We are soul mates, courtesy of Aunt Hena, but why did we want to take each other's clothes off before actually getting to know one another? Doesn't it seem like something else is influencing this attraction we have toward one another?"

Marie was quiet for a moment. "I don't know what it means to be attracted to another. It is something that we familiars do not get cursed with. But, from the way he smelled under all that stench, is desire."

Rising, I ambled over to the window, glancing down at the vacant yard, watching the sun drift to sleep as the moon woke from its slumber.

"Zirena, Hena does not make mistakes. Until you and Dean have the conversation you need to, then the tension will always be there. If you desire to get to know him first, then make it a point to get to know him.

I am here to stop you from sinking your fangs into him." She was right.

"I will see him at dinner, and will talk to him then about having a moment to speak."

"Good, now we need to continue training. You can fight, but you still can't block me from your mind all the way, but that will not happen until you drink. So, let's work on summoning your wings."

"No," I said, turning toward her.

"No?" she purred, raising an eyebrow.

"The last time I had wings, I turned into a beast. I had no control over my actions and almost killed Demetrius. Which, now that I think about it, wouldn't have been a terrible idea." Marie charged at me, pawing my face, gripping her hind claws into my waistband to ensure she didn't fall. I placed my hand under her rear to help hold her.

"Stop this nonsense, Zirena. You are a Skita, the one and only. You are a badass fighter and if you would stop holding back, you could even take down those monsters who killed Rita. So, we are leaving today before the market closes for the night."

"What?" I said, placing her gently atop the wardrobe.

"The king has permitted you to leave the castle as long as you stay within the town. Once I ink on your arm, head out of the castle and go to the market."

"What is the point of this?" I asked as she started sinking back on my arm.

"Move it," she ordered.

"Where are we headed?" Sir Jorah asked as I started walking down the hall toward the exit. They assigned Sir Jorah to me the night of the attack. He is unmarried and young, around the same age as Dean. With his sandy hair, crystal blue eyes, and pale skin, he is quite eye-catching. He always adorns his armor except for a helmet, which is nice when needing someone other than Marie to talk to.

I spent little time outside my room except to tend to the kitchens. Princess Antionette stays with a mistress, so I rarely ever see her unless serving dinner. Once Dean left, the king ordered me to eat with the rest of the servants after I finished serving him.

"I need to go to the market. Is there an artisan's cart? I have had the hankering to draw, but I don't have any supplies."

"Yes." He fell into step beside me, guiding me out of the gates, down the narrow steps, and onto the cobblestone path that leads to the market.

****

"Do you enjoy charcoal?" the craftworker asked me as my fingers brushed against the delicately wrapped fusain sticks finely crafted for sketching.

"Yes," I answered with a smile. My fingers glided to the parchments that were stacked neatly next to them. Some felt normal and crinkled at my touch, most likely made from oak trees—their parchments more nimble than other timber.

"Do you have another kind of parchment style?" I asked, looking into the blue-gray eyes of the old man. His white whiskers nearly covered half of his midnight-colored face.

"No. In times like these, with the way the taxes are, we cannot afford anything better."

"What do you mean by taxes?" His eyes shot behind me, right onto where Sir Jorah was standing. I leaned in so he could whisper.

"The king sends his men to collect taxes. They have increased over the last decade. Many of the families here cannot afford to live."

"What about the prince?"

"We never see him and if we do, the sobs come before he does. Because Prince Dean is here, it means men have died." Tears filled my eyes and anger coursed through my veins again. That bastard king will get what he deserves, and Dean, gods, he doesn't care for these people.

"Zirena, we should head back now," Sir Jorah called from behind. I smiled at the shopkeeper and placed three gold coins in his hand, and thanked him for the charcoal and parchments.

"Draw me something, please," he asked as I walked away. I nodded in response, and he tipped his burley hat toward me.

"What did he say to you?" Sir Jorah asked as we strode through the palace gates.

"Nothing you should concern yourself with."

Gripping my arm tightly, he pulled me to a stop.

"Unhand me." I deliberately glanced around for any other guard to witness what was going on. I could overpower him, but couldn't. The fact that I was stronger than him would reveal my secret.

"Tell me what the old crone said, and I will." Those bright blue eyes leered furiously at me.

"No." With a tug, he pulled me into a broom closet and pushed me against the back wall. Pinning my wrist to the sides of my head, he placed a knee between my thighs. "You bastard. Let go of me before I—"

"Before you what? Tell me, Zirena, did you think I

wouldn't notice your late-night runs? Hear the conversations you have in your room late at night and the weird noises that come from within?" His eyes are scrutinizing me, his face so close to mine. Marie was on my shoulder, hissing, the second he pulled me into the room.

"You need me to claw his eyes out?" she hissed, baring her teeth, both of us knowing he cannot see her.

"What are you?" he asked.

My fangs were out and ready to strike, but I couldn't do it. They remained hidden, mouth shut, while I desperately tried to retract them. Composing myself, I responded.

"I am Zirena, you know who I am."

He remained quiet, eyes fixated on my face. Pressing his forehead into me, his lips mere inches from mine, infuriated me.

"Zirena, you need to get out of this situation. You know what will happen if you don't," Marie hissed. I couldn't answer her without appearing insane to Jorah.

"You are beautiful, Zirena, did I ever tell you that?" His eyes trailed down my body. "Maggie told me you are still a maiden. I could show you how it feels to be with a man."

"Fuck you."

He smiled at me this time. But it was a wicked one.

"Would you like that? I have seen the way you look at me," he started as he placed my wrists together in one hand and started lifting my skirts with the other one. """

Marie's hissing heightened. I had to stop this. Damn the consequences. Before I could sink my fangs into him and push him off me, the door swung open, and someone pulled Jorah off me.

"Your Highness," Jorah started, but it didn't stop Dean's fist from connecting with Jorah's jaw, blood spilling from his face as he fell to the floor.

"Bring him to the dungeons," Dean ordered, as I tried to retract my fangs before someone spotted them. Once the guards left, Dean held out a hand. A friendly gesture, but I didn't take it. Instead, I pushed past him.

"Say something, Zirena," Marie hissed and pawed at me to stop. I turned back to Dean. Instead of saying something, I ran up to him and kissed him. He closed his arms around me tightly, bringing us back into that closet, and shutting the door.

When we broke free from each other, his hands gripped my hips while mine gripped his shoulders. Pressing his forehead into mine, he spoke. "Did he hurt you?" There was fear in those words.

To reassure him, I cupped his cheek and lifted his gaze to mine. "No." But the realization hit me. It was time for him to know the truth. I cannot deny myself to him any longer. "Dean, there is something I need to tell you."

"You don't have to say anything," he said before pressing his lips onto mine, his tongue trying to pierce through, but I resisted because then he would feel them.

"Dean." I moaned as his lips traveled down to my neck. "Dean, listen to me." He broke from my neck, stepped back, and then gestured for me to say what I needed to.

"Before I tell you, I need you to promise me something."

"Zirena, why do I get a feeling this is going to be bad?"

I play with my skirts, picking at my nails. Never have I ever been this nervous. Not for anything.

"Because to you it will be bad, but you have to promise me you will give me a chance and hear me out."

"I promise."

"Thank you, but I also don't think a broom closet is the best place for this conversation," I said as I looked around the dusty shelves.

"Your quarters or mine?" he asked with a wink.

"Mine."

****

My stomach erupted in tight knots as I closed the door behind him. The air has suddenly turned hot, and I look over at Marie, who has sunk back into my skin. For the first time in my life, I am truly afraid.

As he turned to amble toward me, I held out my hand.

"Stop." He did as requested but with a puzzled look etched on his face.

"I need there to be a space between us."

"Okay." Glancing around, he pulled out a chair and sat. Not moving, I swallow my words hard.

"Before I tell you what I need to say to you," —I started moving my hands in nervous circles. I close the gap between us, standing in front of him.— "Promise me you will wait until I am completely done before you decide."

"Decide what?"

"Just promise me, Dean, please?" I took a deep breath, hoping he'd hear the urgency in my voice. Shifting slightly, I glanced down at him, imploring him silently to respond.

"I promise." Before I destroyed everything that we have, regardless of whether it is because of being soul mates, I needed to kiss him one last time before he discovered the monster that I was. Approaching him, I leaned down while cupping his face and planted a kiss on those sinful lips.

"Dean," I backed away from him and started pacing as I spoke. "All my life I have lived with the Immortals on the other side and you and your father want to know why I am still alive and not one of them. Well, I am here to tell you why."

"Zirena, you don't—"

"Don't interrupt me." He apologized, so I continued. "As I was saying. My mother was gifted by our God, Lucan. For reasons I am still trying to understand, he used his blood to bring me to live inside my mortal mother's womb. She died in childbirth, and I was taken by the Immortals to be raised as a weapon.

"That is what Lucan wanted to happen, but they didn't listen. They planned to mate me with one of their own to create a hybrid."

"I saw you twice before I met you. At first, I wanted to kill you, drink your blood, and fuck you at the same time. I stopped myself. The second time, the barrier was between us. I saw you, but I don't think you noticed me." I glanced over at him, trying to read his expression, but I couldn't make it out.

"The day you came for me, we were on our way to Castle Alvion to perform my ceremony with Demetrius. Mortal bandits attacked us and instead of obeying that misogynist bastard, I fought. He strung me up by chains and beat me for it." Dean leaned over with a look of processing my words. "You didn't know it, but I am a half-blood Skita. The real me is a monster with horns, wings, talons, and fangs."

"The closer we got, the instant desire to rip each other's clothes off is because we are soul bound to one another. I stopped every time because when it gets too intense, I come too close to sinking my teeth into you. Your scent is alluring and damning." I look at him. His heartbeat is too calm. There is a scent of that desire and yet something new.

"Why are you telling me this?"

I am taken aback by his question. "What?"

"Why did you choose today to tell me all this?" *Gods.*

"Because I can't deny what I feel around you any longer. My need to taste you, to have you inside of me, is becoming too great, and I need to ask you something." He nods in anticipation. "I want you to choose. I am giving you the choice, Dean. Kill me or love me as I am."

Kneeling in front of him, I look at the floor and wait for his decision.

"What are you doing?" Marie hisses in my ear. Ignoring her, I don't move even as I hear Dean's heart increase its rhythm. A warm, callused hand cups my chin and tilts my head up.

"Show me," he said in a deep and seductive tone. "Show me the real you." Unmoved, he grabs me by my waist, hoisting me onto him as my thighs go to either side of his hips.

"Dean." I gasp as his hand trails down my body and those lips land on my neck.

"Show me who you are, Zirena." Pulling me closer to him, our lips collide, tongues dancing as his hand moves up my bare thigh to the pooled wetness between my thighs. I moan as that deep fire and burning ache to taste him hit me hard. My lips moved to that pulsating vein in his neck. My fangs elongate, not predator-like, but one whose mind was filled with only one thing. The hunger for his blood.

As his tongue continued to lavish my neck, kissing every inch of me with those luscious lips, I suddenly froze.

"Dean," I moaned, pushing his head away to look at me. He stilled, one hand moving over my lips, gently tracing their outline. His pulse doubled in speed, and the smell of lust enveloped me.

"You are not a monster, Zirena. You are beautiful and I will do whatever you need me to do so we can be together. If I have to kill my father to protect you, I will. If I have to burn this world down to protect you, I will."

Gods.

"Dean, I need you to understand that this road will be dangerous. If I bite you, there can be no one else ever."

He gave me his silent response. With a firm grip, he held the back of my neck and tilted his head to the side. "Take whatever is needed for us to be together forever."

As my fangs elongated, he pushed my head toward his neck, and I plunged forward. Warm cinnamon and fire hit my mouth, flowing down my throat as his blood went from him to me. My body was on fire, and the taste, the longing, was too much. My fangs sank deeper as he moaned, hands caressing my body, my breasts... his fingers continuing to pump in and out of me.

"Fuck," he groaned in sheer ecstasy.

Getting to his feet, his hands moved to my rear as he carried me to the bed. The more I drink, the more I yearned. Lying on the bed, my mouth fell back from his throat. I look up and watch the trickle of blood seep from the puncture marks.

My tongue peeked forth, licking the remnants of his blood—the taste of him was powerful. With deliberate movements, he removed his clothes, and the sight of him intimidated me further. My eyes trailed every curve, every scar that flowed down that bronzed body. When they land on his erection, I gasp at the sight of it. Crawling over me, he licked his blood from my mouth and lips.

Those powerful hands moved to my back as he undid the ties, loosening the fabric. He stopped, his eyes devouring me from top to bottom.

"You are so damned beautiful, Zirena." Without a pause, his mouth worships my body from my head to my neck, lingering at my breast. His eyes glance up as he bites down, sucking, leaving his marks on my skin. Then he slowly descends to my sex. Moans escape me as I squirm in pleasure.

"This is fucking better than any dream," I heard myself say.

"Dream?" he questions mid-lap before resuming pleasuring me. Pressure builds in my lower core with his continued ministrations to bring me over the edge.

"Dean, please," I moaned as my hips bucked. My release was swift on his lips, exhilarating, barely able to think with the sensation overpowering me. Panting, I looked down at his glossed lips, and he ran his tongue over them.

"Delicious." He moves over to me, placing the tip at my entrance. "Are you ready?"

"Are you?" I ask, looking into his beautiful eyes. "Are you ready to be mine forever?"

He nudged himself into me. There is burning like before with the speculum, but it isn't enough. I've wanted this for so long. My hands find their way to his butt, and I push him deep inside of me.

"Gods," I moaned. His slow rhythms allow me time to adjust, but I don't want him to slow. "Harder."

As he picks up a rhythm, pumping in and out, I kiss him again.

"Bite me."

I sank my fangs back into him, and the endorphin of our union increased tenfold. He moved faster, harder, gripping a fist full of my hair as I continued to suck his neck. Gods, the sex, the blood, the sheer scent of him was so overwhelming I screamed my release into his neck, and he unloaded his cum at the same time.

A mix of sweat and blood covered our joined bodies. Panting, he is still over me as I look into his eyes, searching for regret, anything to tell me that this was a dream. My gaze drifted to the blood on his neck and my mark.

Reaching out my hand, I caressed his face, down his neck.

"Did it hurt?"

"It was more arousing than it was painful." Rolling off me to lie next to me, he pulled me into him.

"Dean," I started.

"Zirena." I turned to face him. My finger traced along his jawline as he propped himself onto an elbow. "Did I hurt you? I mean, I am your first."

"Am I not your first?" I asked him. If not, I will go kill those other women he has been with. He is mine forever now.

"You are. And my last." He kissed my nose. It was imperative to tell him about the plan to destroy the Immortals. The being that I have to become to kill them all. I didn't want to ruin this moment between us, however, so I remained quiet. Dean soon fell asleep next to me, and I wondered what my bite would do to him. Will he converge into something non-human?

"Well, that was erotic," Marie said, and I flinched. "Did you forget about me?"

"No, I was just caught up in the moment," I whispered.

"You can admit it."

"Admit what?"

"That I was right.

"You drank from him and didn't lose control." She started licking her paw and running it over her ears.

"Whatever. I still want more. I just wanted for him to love me more than I wanted to kill him."

"How do you feel now that you have had your first taste?"

"When his blood touched my lips, it was like warm cinnamon and then heat. Addicting. That is the perfect word to describe it."

"If I had a mate that looked like him, I would be addicted too." I laughed as I threw a pillow at her.

"Can he hear us?" I asked her as he stirred a little.

"Not unless I permit him.

"Just like he can't see me unless I permit him." That was a relief.

"You need to tell him the rest," Marie said after a

few minutes.

"I know. Once he wakes up, I will." I glanced down at him, peacefully asleep.

"I am falling for him, Marie, and I am scared."

"Don't fear love, Zia. Appreciate it, and hold on to it with every breath because it is rare. And remember, Zia, you gave him a choice." She was right.

I allowed him to decide, as much as I believed it would disgust him. He chose me. To be mine and, now, I have to protect him from everything and everyone. Including me.

****

The next day came with the sun peeking through my curtains and Dean's lips on my neck while his hand found its new favorite spot on my body, waking me up in the most wonderful way.

"Good morning, beautiful," he said as my eyes fluttered open and I rocked my hips against him.

"Are you ready for more?"

"Yes," I moaned, and he moved on top of me, not wasting another second before he plunged inside of me while exposing his neck to me. My fangs immediately elongated, eager to taste him once again. His scent was intoxicating, enticing, but I couldn't focus on it with him moving inside of me like that.

"Bitc me." Those words invigorated me. "Please."

That was all it took for me to sink my fangs into him again. Sucking that decadent iron fire into my mouth and down my throat. As I sucked deeper, I moved him onto his back, plunging into him. My hips moved rhythmically to a silent tune playing in my head as I pinned him by his wrists to my mattress. He smiled at me and I leaned down and bit his chest.

He kept moaning my name as my hands traveled from his wrists to his shoulders, his hands placed on my hips, lifting me slightly as he thrust into me. "Play with yourself. I want to feel you cum all over my cock. Clench me and claim it as yours."

His scent is overpowering—lustful. Slick sweat forms on his body. The tempo of my heart increased the harder he thrust into me. I moaned and my hands moved down the front of my body, pinching each raised nipple until finding my clit. I pressed my fingers to his mouth. He sucked them hard, swirling his tongue around them until they were coated with his spit. Once he released them with a nip, I moved them back to my clit and began circling it. Pressing down as he thrust into me. "Faster, Dean. Fuck me."

He picked up his pace, his fingers digging into my hips, and I knew the marks they will leave are ones that I will love for the rest of my life. I added pressure to my throbbing bud as my climax soared, ready to come. I felt him holding back.

"Look into my eyes, Zirena. I want to look into your soul as I claim you as mine."

He sat up quickly, the different angle hitting me in a most delicious way. When he clamped his teeth around my nipple, I screamed during my climax, looking into his eyes before my teeth sank into his neck and claimed his seed inside of me.

"I enjoy being on top," I muttered after catching my breath.

"I like that too." He smiled and placed a chaste kiss on my lips. He eased out of me and swung his legs over the side of the bed. Standing, our grip on each other never faltered as we made our way to the bathing chamber. I set myself down and filled the tub with heated water from the fireplace. Once it steamed, he guided me inside, then nuzzled in behind me. His legs straddled either side of me.

His semi-hard cock pressed into my back. "Dean, are you able to go another round so soon after?"

He chuckled and leaned forward, his lips pressing against my neck before whispering into my ear, "With you, anything is possible." His hands moved down my back, kneading my muscles until he reached my butt. "I want to fill all your holes with my seed." His fingers sank to the tight hole of my ass and circled it, rushing a new feeling of anxiety and arousal rush course through me. "Including this one."

I turned my head around to meet his half-hooded gaze. "Is that what you want? To fill me with your seed in all ways possible?"

I knew I would give this man anything he'd ask for because my heart, my soul, and my body belonged to him. There will never be another that I will want as much as I want him.

"Only if you agree to it," he said.

I reached forward, gripped his cock, and thrummed it up and down. He groaned and grasped my chin, forcing my lips against his while our tongues danced. My hands moved to my sex as I pressed my fingers in and out. "I need you to say it."

"Take me," I answered, and he claimed my mouth again. I pulled my fingers out and then gripped his hand, moving it into my tight hole and pressing the tip of his finger inside. "Oh, fuck."

The burning was more than my sex. It was new, and he drawled.

"We need more than water to help ease my fingers inside of you." Without warning, he stood, water dripping from his body. I watched him exit the tub and walk out into his room. He returned a moment later with something in his hand. "Stand and turn around."

I smiled and did as he commanded.

When he neared, I felt his heat against my back as he pressed a kiss between my shoulder blades. "Spread your legs for me and relax."

I did, the anticipation increasing my heart rate and my fangs tingling. I felt his fingers and something cool circling my hole. It's soothing and when he pressed the tip forward, the pain no longer existed. "This is a salve made from medicinal herbs. It helps numb pain when suturing."

"Why do you have some?" His finger plunged to the knuckle. I palmed the wall.

"I carry it with me, just in case. How do you feel?" A second finger edged inside as he pumped the first. I moaned in response, unable to form words. "I need you to take three before I can fit."

"Yes," I moaned, tensing slightly as two fingers pumped in and out of me. The third is right there, but he was taking too long. "Just do it. I can take it. Make it four because I need to feel you inside of me—"

He plunged all four inside of me, the last of my words turning into a scream that quickly spun into a moan of pleasure. I rocked against his hand, meeting each thrust. My hands move to my clit and finger it. I matched his pace until I am on the edge once more. "Harder, Dean. Make me come and then fuck me."

He let out a raspy groan, gripping my neck to claim my lips again. When my fangs sank into his lips and his blood hit my tongue, I climaxed, clenching around both his hand and mine.

"Fuck. Are you ready to take my cock?"

"Yes." A long, howling pant escaped my lips as he pulled his hand out. I felt the tip of him at my sex. My hand immediately moved away, giving him access to pump into me, covering it with my cum before he pulled out.

When the tip of his cock nudged my hole, I groaned. "Fuck me, Dean."

"I don't want to hurt you," he protested, slowly progressing forward.

"I can take it," I argued in anxious gasps, and he gave me what I wanted. He plunged inside, all the way to the base. We paused to catch our breath.

"So. Fucking. Good. They made you for me, Zirena." He peppered my skin with kisses. My fangs continued to tingle. He placed his arm to my mouth. "Take my blood while I claim your ass."

No prodding was necessary. I sank my fangs into him and he bellied out a moan, pulling out his cock, teasing me, and thrusting back in. The pace was punishing, but each pull of his blood inside of me matched the thrust of his hips behind me. I was stretched and filled with Dean. My new addiction. My favorite drug. All mine.

"Marry me, Zirena," He breathed out mid-thrust, and surprise captured me. But, my answer was more shocking.

"Yes. Fuck, yes, with all my heart I am yours, Dean." He groaned, and I felt him growing bigger, his balls drawing taut, and then he pistoned into me until his hot seed pumped into me. We came down from our high and he eased out of me. I turned to face him, looking into his eyes. "I'm going to marry you, Dean. They mated us for life in my culture, but if marrying you will make me yours in the eyes of the kingdom, then so be it."

"You're mine, regardless of who is looking." He kissed me and we settled into the bath. Kissing, touching, and being with each other until long after, it ran cold.

After we washed and got dressed again, I knew it was time to tell him the rest. As he finished ordering Sir Jorah to send for our meals, I took a seat at the table and waited for him to join me. I wasn't worried about the knight seeing his puncture wounds, because he bore a blouse that covered it to more than an inch.

"What's the matter? Why do you look distressed?" he asked.

"There is more that I need to tell you."

He chuckled. "You mean more than the fact that you are a demi-god vampire?"

"Yes," I stated. "The entire time you were gone, I have been training."

"Training? For what?"

"To kill the Immortal King and Queen and rid the realm of the Immortals." I watched as his brow raised in confusion. He shifted in his seat, and I can tell he wasn't sure how to respond to that. "Dean, I am going to kill them."

"Do you know the one down in the dungeons?"

"He smelled familiar, but I couldn't see him."

"If I take you to him, what will you do?" That was another strange question.

"I'm not sure. I have to know who it is first."

"Would anyone help us with this mission of yours?"

Us? He said, us. I can't let him join me. They will smell my scent on him and know he is mine.

"I don't think so. I didn't have any friends." How do I stop him from coming with me?

"Want to find out?" he asked, getting to his feet and reaching out a hand. I smiled at him as he pulled and crushed me into him.

"Yes." I smiled and then planted a kiss on his lips.

Chapter 15

As we made our way down the spiral stone staircase that lead to the dungeon, I contemplated what I would do once I saw the prisoner. Was it Demetrius or Alec? What about another Immortal like Simon or Tyler? Stepping onto the last step, the prisoner came into view.

Those familiar bright sapphires glared at me through the iron bars.

"Alec," I muttered as I am stunned in place.

"Hello, Zirena." His tone was as cold as the room. "I see you are still alive and," —he sniffs the air, no doubt scenting Dean's mixed with mine.— "you have found yourself a blood bag."

"You don't know what you are talking about," I stammer, approaching him. He lets out a small laugh, glaring his fangs at me.

"I can smell his scent all over you. But flaunting your new mate isn't why you are down here."

"What do you know about me?" I asked, trying to figure out if he was told the same lies as me.

"Besides the fact that you are a disobedient whore." His eyes narrowed, pinning me with a menacing glare.

"Shut your fucking mouth." Dean slammed his sword against the bars, earning another laugh from Alec.

"Pretty boy is a little sensitive, Zirena. I think you would've done better fucking Dem." Dean charged forward, but I stepped between him and Alec.

"Leave," I barked out. But he remained, eyes fixated on the prisoner. His nostrils flared with anger as he fixated a killer stare at Alec. "Dean, leave us, he cannot hurt me."

"If you so much as break a single hair on her body, I will gut you and leave your remains out on display for the rest of your blood-sucking heathens to see what happens when you cross one of us."

"Do as you're told, pet," Alec spat, as my hand wrapped tightly around his neck, digging my nails into it until I felt the blood pebbles. "I see someone has gotten stronger."

"You do not know," I hissed at him, baring my fangs. "Leave, Dean, now." Listening to his footfalls disappear behind me, I glared at Alec.

"How does his blood taste? Does he make you wetter than Dem did?"

"You are disgusting, Alec. Just like the rest of you Immortals." I thrust him back into a wall, stunned momentarily by the obvious evidence of my training. With a loud grunt, he laughed.

Getting to his feet, he spat his blood on the floor. "Does he know the veritable monster you are? I don't mean the fangs, Zirena, but the monster who tore through flesh and bone when the wolves attacked." I braced my ire and remained silent. "No, he doesn't. But if he saw what we saw, your head would be on a spike." He was trying to instill doubt in me, but I told Dean. I gave him the choice. He chose to remain with me.

"Why did you let yourself get captured, Alec? I

know you are smarter than that." Approaching the bars, he gripped them tightly before glaring at me.

"We have been searching for you. Demetrius has been worried sick—"

"Fuck that. You expect me to believe that he cares for me?"

"He is beyond sorry about overreacting."

"Overreacting?" I scoff, letting out a deep, throaty, sarcastic laugh. "Chaining me up and striking me for saving you isn't overreacting, Alec. Gods, how long are you going to get on your hands and knees for him?"

"Zirena, I am serious. Dem loves you and wants you back."

"Well, you and that sadistic asshole can shove it up your asses because I am not going back."

"You will come home, Zirena." He said that as though the choice was not mine to make.

"You are right." He smiled at me. "I will come home, Alec, and when I do, you will know it because every single Immortal will be dead."

"You are not strong enough to kill us all, Zirena." But he didn't know what I was and, now that Dean had given himself to me, I was strong enough to rid the entire world of them.

"You underestimate me, Alec. Just like every one of you has."

"You are right about one thing." He paused, those sapphires staring unafraid. "We underestimate your ability to withstand human blood and dick."

The fire that burned inside of me couldn't be contained any longer. Ripping the bars from their holes, I charged Alec fast. Caught in my rage, I didn't see Marie un-ink herself until she was baring her teeth at the Immortal that I had pinned to the wall.

"You have a familiar?" he asked with widened eyes that stared at the fully morphed Marie. This was the first time I had seen her true form, and it was intimidating. A full-grown saber-tooth tiger with silver fur that glistened in the light of the torches. "I can help you."

"Why would I trust you?" I hissed.

"You want revenge for what the Council did to Rita." How did he know about that? "I know what they have planned. I will help you if your prince agrees to let me live here for the rest of my life."

"How long have you known?"

"About Rita? Or about your true purpose?"

"Both." I maintained my grip on his arm while Marie continued to bear down on him. Waiting for him to try something deadly.

"I will tell you, but first you have to let go of me."

"Don't do it," Marie hissed, her body tense, ready to attack.

"I'm not. Tell me everything before I rip your heart out. You won't come back from that."

He laughed.

"I knew about Rita before they left for the patrols. She was going to tell you everything."

"I already know that, Alec. That's why they killed her."

"Someone has been talking to the gods." He smirked. "I knew about your true purpose as soon as your mother was pregnant with you."

"This isn't helping you, Alec." I dug my nails right into his heart. There was no heartbeat. No pulse. He was dead. Before I could do anything else, I hit the wall hard.

"You may be a Skita, Zirena," he said, smirking, as he approached me. Marie came charging at him, but he gripped her by the throat. "Down, pussycat." The sound of snapping bones and a squeal from her was what I heard before she slumped to the floor.

I froze for a split second, trying to comprehend what just happened. "Nooo," I screamed, watching helplessly as Marie dissipated into dust. "You bastard." Getting to my feet, I desperately tried to summon the beast, but nothing happened. Alec gripped my throat hard, squeezing tightly.

"Demetrius will still take you. *Even* in your tainted form." Lifting me to eye level, I try to fight him, but losing my familiar had sucked the air from my lungs. My entire body shook with rage. Bringing me closer to his face, he sniffed me like the animal he was, then ran a disgusting tongue along my face. "I think I will have you first."

His mouth traveled from my face down to my neck and I felt the scraping of his fangs just before a burning pain scorched me. He bit me. My body went frigid as I felt my blood draining from my body.

"You taste better than you smell, Zirena."

"Fuck you," I muttered weakly.

"Okay." He smirked and removed my breeches roughly. "I know what you were thinking about before you ended up here. I know about the dream you had of Demetrius and the fact that you wanted both of us the same."

"How?" I felt useless, weak, without the ability to call the beast forward. Alec was stronger than me and Marie was dead.

"You don't know me, but you are about to."

I felt him at my entrance and then nothing except the cold stone of the floor. Through blurred vision, I saw Lucan.

His hand wrapped tightly around Alec's bewildered head.

"You will not touch my daughter," thundered Lucan.

Alec struggled to break free, fists pounding away at his assailant. Then his head exploded, blood splattering everywhere.

"Zirena." Dean came rushing in, sword drawn, but Lucan had disappeared.

"I'm sorry," I muttered before my world went black.

My daughter. Lucan called me his daughter.

Snapping awake, I realized immediately this wasn't my room. The bed had emerald sheets and, as I looked around, there were similarities to my room, such as the dresser and table.

Getting to my feet, I walked around, trying to recollect what had happened. Entering the washroom, I looked at my image in the mirror. My floor-length hair was unbraided but washed.

"You're awake."

"Dean." I turned and ran to him, wrapping my arms tightly around his neck. "What happened?"

"You almost died," another voice said. I looked past Dean and noticed Lucan sitting at the table, sipping on a cup.

"Lucan?" I asked, puzzled, as I walked over to him. Then flashes came back to me, making me dizzy. Dean gripped my waist to steady me as I glanced to the side, staring at my bare arm where Marie used to live. "She's dead."

"Unfortunately," Lucan stated, and I detected disappointment and sorrow in his tone. "What were you thinking?"

"I'm sorry. I didn't—"

"Exactly. You *weren't* thinking. Very self-destructive. Marie is dead, you almost died, and he fed on you," Lucan scoffed.

"Don't be so hard on her," Dean said.

"Wait. You can see him?" I asked, pointing at Lucan.

"Of course he can. He is part of the reason you are still alive, regardless of your stupidity."

"What exactly happened?" I asked them.

"Well, you tried to take Alec on by yourself because you thought you were strong enough to take him on. Marie died. He drank from you and nearly raped you. Dean was trying to get back the entire time, but Alec was half-witch and he had put a spell on the door. When the boy prayed, I answered and killed him."

"Alec was half-witch? How is that possible?"

"Honestly, girl, do I need to explain to you what happens when two species mate with one another?" Lucan asked sarcastically.

"You're angry with me," I said. He scoffed in an irate manner. "I did everything you said I was supposed to do. I drank from Dean and trained with Marie the entire time."

"You didn't drink enough," he clapped back, making me shut my mouth. The tension was so high in this room I thought a fire would start.

"How many does she need to drink?"

My head whipped around to glare at Dean.

"It doesn't matter," Lucan said, pinching the bridge of his nose.

"Yes, it does. She almost died, and if we are going to destroy those Immortals, then we need her to be at her strongest." They were talking like they have known each other for a while.

"She will need to bring you beyond death's door."

"No," I said, shaking my head in disbelief.

"Zirena," Dean said, gripping my arm and turning me toward him. He cupped my face and kissed me softly. "It's okay."

"Why would you listen to him? How are you so calm? He is a god, and you are acting like he is just another person." Tears streamed down my face.

"We had time to talk while you were recovering," Dean said.

How long was I out for?

"To answer the question I know you are dying to ask. —You have been unconscious for a week. Lucan gave you blood to help you heal."

"So did Dean," Lucan said.

"I was scared at first when I met him. But he showed me everything. And, Zirena," Dean said as he pulled me into him, "you are the only one who can defeat them, and I want to help. You need my blood to do it."

"I just found you," I said, shaking my head.

"I know, but we will be together again."

Turning my head to Lucan, I saw sympathy on his face.

"Is there no other way?" I ask.

"I'm sorry." Falling to my knees, a flood of tears

tumbled from my eyes. Dean followed suit, holding me to him.

"Look at me," he said, cupping my face and wiping my tears away. "When I leave this world, I will leave it knowing that I met you."

"Dean," I stammered. "I can't lose you." His gaze shifted over my shoulder, nodding to Lucan. I felt the second he left the room.

He kissed me deeply. "You won't. I will be with you the entire time." Without another second, we were kissing again. If he had to die, I would love him one last time. Carrying me to the bed, he explored my body, kissing every inch. Memorizing it as the passion between us exploded, the sensual atmosphere circling the room. Our rhythm was slow, longing, and heart-wrenching because a moment like this only comes when the end is near.

"I'm ready." He looked at me with composure, and commitment. While I continued to move my hips on him, I sank my fangs into his neck. Drinking that cinnamon fire into me. As his blood pooled inside of me, my tears fell. His hold on me faltered and he fell into unconsciousness beneath me.

It was gone. The pulse that called to me for so long was now flatlined. The warmth he had once displayed had disappeared looking down at him.

Dean was dead.

The entire castle shook by my blood-curtailing scream as arms and blankets wrapped tightly around me.

"I'm sorry, Zia."

"I love him," I barely whispered from sorrow.

"I know." Lucan held me in his arms.

****

The smoke from the pier filled the air as I stared down at Dean's burning body, his blood still warm inside of me, fueling the power within. Tonight, I will attack those that betrayed me, lied to me, and took those I loved most from me. Tonight, the Immortals will find out who I am and regret the day they defied the gods.

"Are you ready, Zirena?" Lucan asked from behind me as I strapped daggers to both of my thighs. I fastened my hair into two long braids just like always when I was ready to fight. Dressed in all black, closing my eyes, I suppressed the pain of Dean's death and allowed the rage to take over.

The crunching of my back sounded just before my wings broke free. Looking at my hands, my once-clear nails are now long talons that look just like a hawk's. From my head, two horns shoot out like two sharpened spikes. My fangs remained elongated as I turned to look at him.

"I'm ready." Without another word, I fly through the opened window, watching the skies crossing over the sleeping village and the vast evergreens on the other side of the barrier.

With each flap, a gust of cold air touched my skin. Flying was new, exciting, and natural. The wind was like an old friend as it assisted me to soar in my journey across the sky.

You aren't a monster; you are beautiful. Every memory of Dean flashed through my head. My skin longed to touch him again as his blood coursed through my veins.

Over the peak of the treetops, I see the erect top of a pointed staff sticking out of the top of one of the triangular towers. Castle Alvion entered my line of sight with each passing of the forest below.

Six vast, triangular towers overshadow the skyline of this massive fortress, connected by reinforced, rock-solid walls made of sandstone. Tall, wide windows are scattered = across the walls in a distorted pattern, along with proportional holes for archers and artillery.

With wings tucked in, I swoop in through a vacant hole—an easy entry. Crouching low, I peek out but see no one nearby. Running, I find another vacant tower with one door that has a spiraling staircase. Cautiously, I make my way down, unsheathing my daggers preparing for a fight, but nothing and no one comes.

At the end, another wooden door appeared. It seemed too quiet. Closing everything else nearby, I tuned in to the sounds of the castle but heard nothing or anyone.

Perplexed, I sped-ran to the throne hall. It was as vacant as the rest of the castle. *Where is everyone?*

"Look at you."

I turned at the sound of a familiar voice.

"Demetrius," I hissed, both daggers raised and poised to use.

"Even in your full demonic form, you are still arousing."

"You're disgusting."

"Not as disgusting as a human's whore. Where is your lover, by the way?" Demetrius eyed me from head to toe as he circled me. "You smell of him."

"Where is everyone?" I kept my eyes and daggers at him.

"Hunting." He gave her a wary glance. "You know, we could've been great together, Zirena. But you chose human filth over me." I searched the area for any other sign of another. "I wonder, how did he taste before you drained him dry?" One eyebrow rose as he continued to stare at me.

"How do—"

"I can smell his blood running through yours. Did you think my father wouldn't have told me about you? Why do you think they matched us together?" I didn't answer him because I had no clue. "Because on the night of the ceremony, I was going to fuck you and drink your blood. Transforming *me* into the ultimate weapon."

"You will get nothing from me."

"You don't get it." He snapped his fingers, and I was rushed by two guards. Slicing against them, my blade connected with their necks. Blood splattered the ground. "It's good to know you didn't become rusty while being on your back for that human."

Charging at him, sparks ignited by our clashing blades. He smirked, tilting his head as though to congratulate my move. Kicking my leg out, I swept his feet from under him.

With a hard thud, he landed on the floor. I leaned forward, my blade against his throat, and I spat on him.

"Goodbye, Demetrius." Before I could move my blade, it wrapped tightly around a chain that swirled me.

"Welcome home, Zirena." Turning my head, the entire Council, followed by the queen and king, walked in. Two guards helped Demetrius to his feet.

"You are all going to die," I yelled, tone hardened by fury.

"You had your chance, but you failed again," Lord

Channey spoke. "Chain her up. It's time for her Matching Ceremony." Iron clasped both my wrists and ankles before I could react, spreading them wide, and connected to two posts for a stronghold. Pulling my arms toward me, the resistance was too much. Strength evaded me. *Lucan, you bastard. I did what you asked.*

"Prepare her."

I hissed at my assailants as my clothes were cut from me, exposing me fully to the entire room. "Demetrius will have the first taste of her. Enjoy, my son."

Demetrius prowled toward me. I struggled against the chains, steeling myself against his imminent attack. "This night was supposed to be too private and pleasurable."

He cupped my sex, sliding a finger inside of me. "Lucan," I yelled.

Demetrius smirked while another finger traced the outline of my mouth.

"Lucan is asleep. But keep screaming, I like it." He dropped his breeches, removed his dagger, and slashed my forearms. His mouth closed around my dripping blood. After several swallows, he moaned.

"How does she taste, my son?" Lord Channey asked, licking his lips, euphoria plastered across his face.

"Join me, Father." He gestured toward the man. Both father and son sank their fangs into me as acid burned and slithered its way through my body. Their venom threatened to overtake Dean's blood. I was useless. *I killed the love of my life for this?* To be assaulted and drained? *This isn't how it ends.* As Demetrius thrust inside of me, I screamed. And I screamed again until the entire castle shook by its foundations.

My skin felt like it was on fire. Suddenly, my attackers lessened their hold on me. I watched through clouded vision the Immortal Father and Son suddenly turn to ash. The iron chains clanged to the ground. I was freed.

Someone yelled, "Run." They didn't get far. Rage took over, and I sliced through skin, bone, clothing, and anything that stood in my way. Their blood coated me as I continued to plow through each one. I didn't stop with them. Using the power gifted by my father and my lover, I hunted each Immortal down, decapitating them in my wake. Their mistake was to have thought me weak. Rita's death was finally avenged.

A week later, I sat on the top of the fortress of Alvion. The blood of my enemies remained coated on me.

"You completed your mission." Lucan appeared before me.

"Bring him back," I croaked.

"I can't."

"Bullshit. If you can let your daughter become a monster, you can bring him back," I yelled.

"Zirena, I tried to come before they—"

"Demetrius was inside of me," I babbled. "That coldness is suppressing Dean's warmth. The hate is overtaking the love."

"I can't bring him back. That is beyond my abilities."

"I did everything you asked of me. I did everything they asked me to do, and what do I get? Huh? To live eternity alone as a monster?" Agony flared.

"No, Zirena." I felt him near just as the cold still blade sliced across my neck. My body shattered from shock.

"Why?" I barely croaked out, looking up at him.

"Because I can't make the same mistake twice."

I saw it now. My body lying in his arms as my blood spilled out of the wound from my neck.

Stand up! Come on!

My body refused to obey.

Part Three—Happily Ever Afterlife
Epilogue

A soft hand gripped my shoulder. Turning around, I see him smiling at me in a glowing ambiance.

"Dean?" I wrapped my arms tightly around him.

"Welcome to eternity, Zirena." Dean turned me around to face a vast gilded castle with six slim square towers that were connected by heavy walls made of golden marble.

Someone had perfectly aligned clear windows down the center of each wall in a fairly symmetrical pattern, along with asymmetric crenelations for archers and artillery.

Why would they need that here?

"Dean, how is this possible? I mean…" I paused, looking back at him, still delightfully shocked to be in his arms again.

"This was set forth by the gods and goddesses. Now, this is where we shall spend all of our days. Create our family and live happily ever after." He smiled and my cheeks instantly heated with a strange new feeling. Happiness.

He kissed me quickly. "Come, I need to show you the city."

"City? Why would there be a city in the afterlife?" I asked, confused.

He pulled me through the arched threshold and onto a path.

"Every realm has a society, Z. This is the city of Shimmer and they built it at the edge of a bright, small forest, and is truly an ancient city." I glanced over to the spot he was pointing to, continuing to follow him with our fingers interlaced and soaking in as much information about this world as I can. It was still surreal to be walking beside him.

"It's very charming and is matched by the backdrop of majestic forests which have helped shape the city into what it is today," he said.

"Dean, how do you know all this? You were..." I paused, not wanting to speak those words in the same sentence as his name *ever* again.

"Dead? It's okay, Z. Here, nothing else matters because we get to be free from everything and just live our lives without the pressures of good and evil. We can just...be." He sighed, and I noticed how much he appeared to be at peace. It warmed my heart to see him like this. "I've been here for a while, so once I got over the shock and awe, I explored and spoke with the others living here. They were very informative."

As we continued to make our way into the city, we came across a shop that had the sign *Scholars House* hanging just above the front door. It was beautiful, warm, and smelled of the evergreens back on earth. Scrolls and books with no end in sight were stacked on shelves upon shelves.

"It's an illusion, my dear. You ask me what you want to know and the knowledge presents itself." An older-looking woman stood behind a counter pushed against a small window. Her voice sounded old, but her body appeared to be young. "Since you're new, I'm sure you would like to know a little more about this world, correct?"

I nodded.

A second later, a vast scroll flew across the room and landed on the desk, unrolling itself right in front of me. I read it.

"Everything has a part to play. All the buildings are made from the materials these forests bring in, but they were also influential with architectural designs, as the vast majority of buildings have been built alongside the trees and often incorporate many unique elements."

"Let's explore. Can we take this with us?" Dean asked.

The woman nodded. "It knows when to return."

We exited the store, and I looked up, noticing the modest houses scattered across the skyline, showing what they represented to the city itself. Life was glorious in Shimmergarde and it has attracted a lot of attention. I looked back down at the parchment and read out loud. "Many cultures have left their mark not just on the architecture, but also upon the city's identity. What historically was a city of no variation has grown into a new culture of variety and it's this that unites the over three-thousand people to this day. Isn't that insightful?"

Dean chuckled beside me. "What else does it say?"

"Well, there are a lot of distinct elements, some from the Mayans, Angelo Saxons, and even a place called England. I never knew places like these existed."

"I think the world is a lot bigger than Camilion and Alvion."

"I wish we would've gotten to see it all."

"Perhaps the gods will grant us the honor." He wrapped an arm around my shoulders and held me closer as I let the scroll back up. It slipped from my grip and flew back to where it belonged.

"Magic. It's very exciting," I said.

"Would you like to see the gardens?"

I nod because I am intrigued to think about anything else. I know this should've been a more intimate reunion, but something about this world tells me we will have plenty of time for those things.

When we step up to the glasshouse with the sign Orchid on it, I see plots of fresh grass bordered by thriving flower bushes and shrubs. A single apple tree stands in the front left, its leaves and branches are full of green and red fruit, and nests, some abandoned, others very much alive. The flower beds appear well-kept, precisely cut, and meticulously looked after; they're home to many lives. The rose bushes and shrubs reach five feet high, but this appears deliberate, as they grow along two metal posts. Here and there lie smaller beds, offering a glimpse of the lilacs and daisies. Grape vines eagerly creep and crawl their way beyond their allocated garden spots, each eager to take just a little more land for themselves.

"That apple tree has stood there for a dozen years, and claimed this land first, and they later built the surrounding garden," said a loud male voice coming from directly behind us. *It's no wonder this tree is the biggest eye-catcher.* "The flower beds attract some attention, and the flower bushes and shrubs make sure they're paid attention to as well, but nothing beats the majesty of the tree."

"It's a beautiful tree. Very fruitful," I comment and Dean chuckles beside me. The old man raised a brow, unamused at my attempt at humor.

"Would you like to take some?" he asked, offering an empty basket.

"Thank you," Dean answered and took the basket.

While Dean picked the fruit, I am tempted to ask this man more about this society.

"Sir."

"Call me Boles," he said.

"Mr. Boles."

"No, just Boles."

"Apologies. Boles. I'm new here and I was wondering what your opinion of this place is? The people? Do you see the gods or goddesses ever walking around?"

He gave me an annoyed look before sighing. "This nation is full of cunning, conniving, and intelligence. We have a certain taste for magic and science that none of us were privy to down below."

"Science?" That puzzled me.

"Come. Let me show you." I followed the imp down the rows of the garden until we landed at the back where a well sat. "Look inside and tell me what you see."

I looked inside the shimmering water and saw nothing, at first. Glinting golden flakes glowed beneath the surface and an electric surge pulsed from it. It reminded me of a heartbeat. I reached out and touched it; the essence kissing my skin before sinking into it. My body crunched, and I felt it. The Skita was trying to take form.

Jerking my hand back, I calmed my breathing and met Boles' gray eyes. "Magic calls to magic. Whatever you were on earth, the magic will awaken up here."

"It can't. I was a monster," I whispered, still trying to figure out what had just happened.

"Ready to go?" Dean appeared next to us, holding

a filled basket, and once his eyes noticed my feared expression, he instantly grew concerned. Rushing over to me, he cupped my cheek. "What happened? Did he hurt you?" he demanded.

"No. He just showed me the power of this place. I need to get out of here." There was no hesitation with my request and we said our goodbyes before exiting the garden and headed further into town, down the path leading to the castle gates.

"Do you want to talk about?" he asked after a few minutes of walking had lapsed.

"The magic in that well started awakening the Skita in me. I almost lost control."

"Well, you didn't."

"That's not the point, Dean. I thought that after everything, I would finally get rid of the monster inside of me," I confessed, feeling the prick of angst coursing through me. He looked at me like I was crazy. "I sacrificed you and killed all of them. I did every damn thing Lucan asked of me, and I still end up with this thing inside of me. What if I lose complete control and start killing all these people?"

He chuckled. "You can't kill anyone, Z. We are all already dead. This is the afterlife."

"What if you're wrong?"

He placed a kiss on my forehead. "I might be. The only way to find out is if someone gets stabbed or something. Relax. You're supposed to be stress-free here. This is where we find peace, together."

He was right, but that didn't ease my worry.

I gripped the back of his neck and kissed him deeply, pressing my tongue into his mouth and moaning at the taste of him. We broke our kiss, and he smirked at me. "I love you, Z. But now I need to show you how to relax. Which is why I've brought you to the Tavern."

"What?" I smiled and looked at the place.

From the outside, it appeared cozy, rustic, and enchanting. Tree logs and intricate stone carvings made up most of the building's outer structure. I was able to see through the large, open-curtained windows, but the laughter from within was felt outside. As we entered the tavern through the hard wooden door, the aromas of roasted meats and ale welcomed me. My tension eased.

There was a worker engaged in a conversation, but he took the time to welcome us with a wink. We sat and two mugs appeared in front of us. The sweet scent of peaches wafted from the liquid in my cup. "Cheers, Z. To everlasting love."

"Cheers." We clinked our mugs and drank. The flavor was unlike anything I had ever tasted before. Sweet and tangy, with a hint of alcohol that burned my chest. "I love it."

"Good. This is where we will stay until we relax you enough for me to take you back to our room and have my way with you." He winked and little flutters took flight in my stomach while my sex throbbed with anticipation. I hadn't thought about sex since he died.

As he chatted about his time here, I continued to admire the inside of the building.

It was just as lovely inside as it was on the outside. Tree logs supported the upper floor, and the chandeliers attached to them. The walls were barren, though whether that was the owner's choice or the gods, I'm not entirely sure.

The tavern was packed. After Lifers were the primary clientele here, which made sense. There was no need for money, and that would be another advantage of living in this realm. "Do all the workers volunteer?"

"Not exactly. Since there is no need for money. We all have a job that is assigned to us. They will assign yours tomorrow." He smiled. What could I possibly do? I was a prisoner and a monster. "Don't worry, Z. Whatever it is, I know you will love it."

I took another long drink from my cup and felt a buzz inside my head. Looking around at the several long tables occupied by what appeared to be entire families, all enjoying the food, drinks, and the company of each other. *Everyone is so happy. I can be happy too.*

People are clearly having a good time at all the tables, even the smaller ones. Even most of the stools at the bar were occupied, though nobody seemed to mind more company.

"You look beautiful, Z," Dean said, and I realized he was standing in front of me, with a hand outstretched. "Dance with me?"

I smiled as he whisked me off my feet. A bubble of laughter escaped my lips. "Keep charming me like this and you might find me warming your bed tonight," I whispered in his ear before nipping it.

He groaned and gripped my hips tighter before kissing me deeply. He broke our kiss momentarily to lean forward and whisper back, "Tonight, I'm ravishing you. But tomorrow, I will make love to you. And then, whenever we want, this world is ours to fuck anywhere we please."

"Then take me right here and now," I challenged.

He glanced at me from head to toe, the heat from his lust-filled eyes causing my skin to rise and my sex to throb. "Come with me."

He didn't give me much of a choice as he pulled me toward a small area at the back where more doors were situated. He gripped one and yanked it open before shoving me inside. The lock turned, and he faced me, prowling toward me, causing me to take several steps until my back hit the wall.

"I've waited for you for so long, Z. If this is what you want right now, then tell me with your words. Do not tease." His stare was so intense as he reached out and ran his fingers down the valley of my breasts. I looked down and realized I was only in my tunic, pants, and boots. My breathing hitched when he ran his fingers down the middle of my sex, teasing my clit, and I was instantly wet. "Well?"

"Yes, Dean, I want you to fuck me."

His heated gaze met mine, and our lips crashed against each other in a deep, hungry kiss. I ripped our clothes from our bodies, and when his mouth clamped down on my nipple, I moaned. My fingers raked through his hair while he marked me. His free hand moved to my aching core, and those tantalizing fingers ran up and down my slit before inserting one finger and palming my clit.

"No teasing. I want you inside of me," I growled and gripped his cock, pumping it up and down.

"We have time, Z. I want to enjoy this," Dean said, continuing to suck on me. I used my speed and took control of the situation.

Pinning him to the wall, one hand wrapped around his wrist, and pinned it above his head. I lined my entrance up with the head of his cock and sank down before he had a chance to object. We both moaned, and I rode him like there was no tomorrow. Bloody hell, this felt good, needed.

"Fuck, Zirena. You feel so good."

"You died. I killed you. Now that I have you, I don't ever want to stop loving you," I confessed. Our lips collided as our bodies continued to mold in heated passion.

****

I woke up to a soft breath that kissed my right cheek.

Turning on my side, I watched as Dean slept peacefully, my ears tuned into the calm beating of his heart. The sound I thought I'd never get to hear again.

I reached out and cupped his cheek; the movement caused him to stir. When his green eyes meet mine, the basic instinct to claim each other took over once more.

Dean hooked an arm around my waist, pulling me against him. A growl of sexual hunger escaped my lips.

He pushed me onto my back and teased me with his erection.

"You want to fuck me, Zirena?" he asked with the same hunger in his eyes I must have projected. "Haven't had enough of my cock?"

I smirked at him, gripping my knees and pushing them apart with a purposeful slowness that made his pulse hammer.

"I love you, Dean. But I have an issue with you teasing me, especially after I had to kill you. I thought I would never see you again and now that I am here with you in the flesh, I never want to stop loving you. Connecting with you each time you thrust into me, filling me with your seed and hoping one day we will conceive."

"I haven't forgotten, Z. This isn't me being spiteful

hoping to wound you," he said softly. "You are mine, Zirena, and nothing you ever do will make me think anything less of you."

My grip on my knees tightened, making my flesh ache for more as I pushed my legs further apart.

"Make love to me. Don't tease me. Prove to me just how much you fucking love me."

"With pleasure," he growled, staring into my eyes.

"Now, Dean. Make me scream your name as you claim me."

He plunged deeper into me and gave me exactly what I asked for. Pumping in and out of me, thrusting fast just the way I liked it. This was the way we were choosing to reconnect. Yet, it didn't feel just physical, but emotional and solely. Just as soul bonded is.

My soul resonated with the bond between us, recognizing him by the way our eyes locked, lips merged, and bodies moved in synch. My thighs clenched and trembled, ready for my release. Everything building up to the moment of our climax was perfect in every way.

With a heavy, satisfied breath, he eased out of me and flopped onto the mattress, pulling me against him. His fingers traced delicate circles across my cheek, tucking strands behind my ear. I feared for an instant this was all a dream and I would wake back up on that rooftop, covered in blood, alone, wishing him alive once more.

"This is real, Zirena. I'm here." He reached for my hand and placed it over his beating heart. "Bite me, taste how real I am."

My fangs tingled with the need, and the sweet, intoxicating scent of his blood enticed me to move forward. Kissing along his jawline, I found his pulsing vein and sank into it. Cinnamon and fire, just as I remembered, and I moaned with the intoxicating flavor as I drew his essence into me.

When my fangs retracted, I licked my lips, savoring his taste before meeting his gaze once more.

"This is real. We're living in the afterlife, together."

"It is. And there is more." He tossed the sheets to the side and jumped from the bed. "Let's get washed and dressed. I will give you a tour."

"How long were you here? It was like a couple of days back on earth," I asked while making my way to the bathing chamber. I stopped at the threshold and gasped at the sight. They made everything out of thick marble, and the picket was golden. "What is this?"

He wrapped his arms around my waist. "This is what they call indoor plumbing. A perk for the dead."

He released me and made his way inside, turning the knobs. I cupped my mouth at the sight of clear water running out of the golden head. "And a couple of days to you were more like a couple of months to me. Time works differently, it would seem."

"This is amazing." I started walking over to the tub, running my fingers in the warm water.

"Now, lilac or cucumber?" he asked, holding up the crystal vases to fill them with purple or green liquid. "Cleaning soaps."

"Both."

"Good choice."

We stepped into the tub and Dean massaged my head and muscles, running his fingers through the floor-length hair, ensuring every inch was cleaned with the cucumber soap. After rinsing my hair, he picked up the lilac and washed me. Slowly and meticulously. It reminded me of the last bath we had together and my thighs clenched. *No more sex for at least a day.*

Once we are both washed and dried, he handed me clothes and footwear. The white dress covered my shoulders halfway and flowed down into a beautiful keyhole neckline. It was a relaxed fit that made the dress feel comfortable, yet elegant. It covered my arms just below my shoulders, which not only helped complement my gorgeous skin, but it also kept the focus on other parts of the dress. Below the waist, the dress fit snugly around me and had a tulip style. The dress reached well above my ankles and was slightly longer at the sides. My shoes were open toes, gorgeous on their own, an ideal match to complement the dress.

They dressed Dean in a smooth tunic and buttoned it up fully to support the elegant tie he was wearing. On top of the shirt, he wore a classy vest with four golden buttons. It had a fairly deep v-line, just narrow enough for the top to remain visible, adding another layer to the overall look of the suit. The jacket was clearly made for him—a perfect fit. It was a simple beige color, giving the suit a dignified and elegant look. The five buttons of his double-breasted jacket were all buttoned up. His pants, which were the same color as the jacket, had a slightly unique pattern. A white pair of boots complemented the entire outfit.

"Why do I feel like they dressed us for a ceremony?" I asked while he held my hands.

"Because we are." He smiled, releasing my hands, and reached into his pocket, grabbing something. Smiling, he held out a glinting golden ring with a diamond at the center. "I asked you to marry me a while ago. I mean, when we were both on earth, you said yes then and I'm hoping you will still say yes today."

I looked at the ring, my heart beating a thousand miles a minute, and without a thought, I answered him. "Yes. Of course I will still marry you."

He slid the ring onto my left ring finger, and then kissed me.

"Come, tour first, then the wedding."

"What? You mean now?"

"Why wait?" He chuckled, dragging me along down the hall.

We rushed down the chamber. I am dragged through dual gates and into a vast room.

"Dean…this, it's magnificent." I glanced at the minutiae that have been presented for the wedding.

"Wait right here. I will meet you at the altar." He releases my grip, and I observed in amazement, elation, and sheer awe at what I saw before me.

Huge braziers enclosing each of the eight ivory columns light up the integrated area and paint the chamber in warm yellows. Gems of the many artworks on the bowed ceiling dance in the flickering light while white roses and statues look down on the maple floor of this majestic hall.

An ivory rug filled with red rose petals are scattered down from the altar for a few meters before ending at my feet. Matching emblems with adorned sides swung from the walls. Between each banner are several candles in small lanterns. Many of them have been lit and illuminated by the portraits of gods and goddesses below them.

They hung drapes from vast windows, colored the

same ivory as the streamers. The curtains are adorned with fine arrangements and fancy tassels.

A ceremonious arch of gold surrounded a giant painting of the realm. The arch, shrouded in tangled sequences and fixed on each of the frontal legs, is a bedecked dragon.

People were waiting for the ceremony to begin, standing, with all eyes centered on me.

As if I didn't think it would get any more perfect, a recognizable purr and the brushing of whiskers came from my right shoulder. "Are you ready, Zirena?"

"Marie? I thought… How?" I stuttered in disbelief while looking into her bright eyes.

She placed the pad of her paws on either side of my face. "This is the afterlife, my dear. All dead things come here. Now, are you ready to marry your soulmate?"

A huge smile lifted the corners of my mouth and I placed a kiss on her forehead, between her eyes. "More than ready."

She jumped from my shoulder, landing on four strong paws in her full silver tiger form. I nodded to her and then she gestured for me to turn around. "Another recognizable face. Who else could—"

I froze the minute I looked at who stood behind me.

"Hello, Zirena. I've been waiting for you." I had heard her cries, had smelled her body change to ash, and my heart had shattered the day she was lost to me. With open arms, I rushed into her embrace, sobs leaving me. "I know, my girl. I know. Nobody will ever come between us again."

Lifting my head to meet her eyes, I beamed with

happiness. "Rita, I'm so sorry."

"Shh. You have nothing to apologize for. Everything I did was to protect you. You weren't responsible for the crimes of those beasts. I would do it all anew." She smiled and wiped the tears from under my eyes.

"I heard you die. I never thought I'd see you again." I kept gazing at her, absorbing the fact she was here with me.

"I know, but here we are and I am so proud of you."

I wrapped my arms tightly around her again. Pressing a kiss on her cheek, I then stepped back.

"Will you walk me down the aisle?" I asked, holding out the crook of my elbow.

"I would be honored, but that position is reserved for your father."

"My father?" My brows knitted with confusion and then I remembered who that was. Images of his hand pressing the blade to my throat. Choking on my blood and then I saw him.

"Hello, daughter. Don't you look beautiful?" he said with a smirk while adjusting the middle button on his silver suit.

Anger burned hot underneath my skin and I felt my Skita breaking through as I charged at him. Claws slashing but failing to connect with him as he dodged my attacks. No one dared to move to stop me.

"You did this to us!" I exclaimed, growling, and then my wings burst from my back, tearing my dress. The sounds of bones crunching and fabric tearing rang incessantly in my ears as I continued my attack on the man who betrayed me.

"Gain control of your Skita, Zirena!" Rita exclaimed as I swiped my right hand at the god, but nothing seemed to faze him. With each move I made, he dodged it. "Zirena, today is your wedding day. Remember, this is your happily ever after with your soul mate."

Lucan's eyes bore into mine, and I glared at him.

I blinked twice as I thought about Rita's words. Today was about Dean and me. No one else mattered and I would not let this god ruin it for me. Or allow me to ruin it.

Reining in my control, I felt the Skita recede into my body as my normal form returned. Looking down, my clothes were torn, and a sigh escaped my lips.

"No worries. The dress will be good as new in three…two…one."

I looked down as Rita's countdown ended and watched as the dress repaired itself.

"How?"

"Magic," Lucan answered, and I snapped my gaze toward him. "I guess now is not a good time to offer my hand down the aisle?"

"No. Rita will walk me, seeing as she is the one who raised me." I turned my back on him to face the woman I've known all my life as more than a friend or mentor. "Rita, it would be an honor for you to walk me."

"I would be delighted." Our elbows interlocked as music played and my heart thundered in my chest.

Today was a day I never thought would come.

As I stared at Dean, my life finally felt as though it was beginning. Without the worry of oppression, murder, or death. This is where I am.

This was our Happily Ever After.

Conclusion

The prince and the Skita start their happily ever after in the wondrous afterlife full of joy and life. Living their life under the roof of the palace as the lord and lady of the castle. The birthright of the Skita. Her father, Lucan, made his amends by granting the Skita the ability to bear children with the prince. When their first of five children was born, a beautiful black-haired baby boy, Lucan blessed him with the gifts of night and day. To walk amongst the humans but have the abilities of the gods; just as he once gifted the Skita.

Throughout eternity, the prince and the Skita watched their children grow in their abilities and intelligence.

When the oldest son, the second born, visited his grandfather, he sought permission to visit the human world, and, by the power of the gods, it was granted.

The heirs of the prince and the Skita were each given free rein to portal to and from the mortal realm so long as they followed the rules set forth by the gods.

If there was any violation, then the rights would be revoked for all five children. Azula, Bailinor, Castian, Deirdre, and Ethena.

For centuries, the children followed the rules, until one didn't.

But, that is another story for another time.

Bonus Content: Azula

Twenty-Years Later

Two million years for humans

Humans have evolved in the past two millennia.

My curiosity increases with the passing day I watch over them. Grandfather Lucan's position he bestowed upon me as the first-born daughter of the goddess of Night & Day.

It's a simple role. Goddess of War and Prophecies. It's my job to prevent unnecessary bloodshed for the mortals. But at times, humans make it difficult to stay impartial. Keeping my distance from them helps suppress the turmoil of emotions of witnessing their selfish tendencies. Grandfather says that's the human in me. I haven't had a vision or prophecy still to this day.

"How are the mortals fairing on this day, Azula?" Mother's voice filters in through the noise of my thoughts, snapping my attention from my looking glass to her.

"Everything is fine, Mother. Is there something that you need from me?" I ask, astutely.

She smiles softly before the tapping of her heels brings her to stand in front of me. We are the same height. My eyes are different from hers. One a blue-gray and the other green-gray. "Your name day celebration is tonight. Are you excited? Perhaps you will meet your match," she says suggestively.

I bit my tongue, preventing myself from cutting my eyes at her. There is nothing I despise more than putting on a gown too big for me and heels that prevent me from carrying my daggers. "Of course, Mother. But if I don't find my match, it will not be the end of the world."

"I see. Az, your father and I only want for you to be happy. And Grand–"

"Grandfather wants me to do my job," I snap. Her expression falters into a frown. Swiping a hand down my face, I pinch the bridge of my nose before stepping away from her. "I will see you tonight."

Escaping to my bathing chamber, I turn the lock and wait for her receding footsteps and the closing of the door. Letting out a breath of air, I move over to my mirror and sigh. My black hair is tied in a tight bun at the back of my head, just as I always have it. "There will be no matching tonight. I will show up for five minutes and then disappear."

A useless pep-talk.

A thought crossed my mind.

What if I escaped to the human world tonight? Say I have a mission to prevent some war from happening. I brushed away the thoughts from my mind just as an image began to form in the looking-glass hanging on my wall. The clear swirling into color, shadows, then images of a human walking down a narrow alley at night.

There is snow covering the ground, and a unique smell of sewer, cooked meat, and smoke engulfs him. I watch as he makes his way around a dimly lit corner, confused at what the mirror is showing me until I hear it. The footfalls of multiple people behind him. He glances over his shoulder, the street signs titled Grover Place and Front Street coming into view as his pace increases slightly. I sniff but smell no fear coming from him. But the foul taste of wolf dances on my tongue. At that moment, I see their luminous eyes glowing with dark intent at their target.

My gaze shifts back to him.

He'll never make it.

Run. I scream, but there's no sound.

The thrumming in my chest matches the crescendo of their steps. Their howls of excitement echo as they close in on their prey.

I have to do something. To stop them. To protect him.

Moving to reach forward to portal myself to the other side, something grabs my hips, jerking me backward. The vision is lost and I push myself away from… "Grandfather? Why did you stop me? That human was in danger."

"Because, child, it is the rules." He sighs, shaking his head.

"Rules? I have not heard of that one. I thought it was my job to prevent the slaughter of innocents?" I ask, crossing my arms over my chest, and leaning against the sink.

"No, dear. Your job is to prevent war and report any prophecies that you have to me so that I may interpret them."

"Was that a prophecy? Or something conjured by my looking glass?"

Grandfather sighs once more before gesturing for me to follow him out into my main living area where my gifted looking glass is mounted. There is nothing else in here aside from my bed and wardrobe. I like the simplicity of it.

"Look here, Azula," he states while swirling his extended claw through the misted water. "What do you see?"

I grip the sides, concentrating on the pool before me. "Nothing."

"What do you feel?"

"Nothing."

"You can neither see nor feel anything from this magically infused looking glass. Created specifically for you to watch over humanity and complete your job as the Goddess of War and Prophecies. Whatever that was in there was a trick. Done by one of your younger siblings, I assume." He flicks a piece of invisible dust from his shoulder. Grandfather always wears a suit. I've never seen him without one. The colors range from gray to black.

"It didn't feel like a prank. Besides, none of them are tricksters. Only an angel can pull something like that off," I state.

"Azula, leave it alone," he insisted.

"But, it's my job—"

"I know what your job is!" he yells. I flinch in shock because he's never lost his temper like this before. "Leave this alone, Azula." His tone is softer this time. "Get ready for your celebration and speak nothing more about what you thought you saw."

I nod to appease him, but once he is gone, I rush back to my bathroom mirror and touch it. Using my powers to summon the portal to where I saw the human last. Electricity coursed through my veins as my head jerked back with my essence pouring into the looking glass. When it shows him once more, I see his back pressed against a metal fence, all four wolves closing in on him.

Now's the time for not second-guessing.

I jump.

A word about the author…

C. M. Hano is a Fantasy Romance Author who aspires to write strong female driven, hot and magical adventures, and being a good mother. She lives in Louisiana with her husband and two daughters.

Thank you for purchasing
this publication of The Wild Rose Press, Inc.

For questions or more information
contact us at
info@thewildrosepress.com.

The Wild Rose Press, Inc.
www.thewildrosepress.com

www.ingramcontent.com/pod-product-compliance
Lightning Source LLC
Chambersburg PA
CBHW060113260626
47160CB00005B/1879